Nanny for My Billionaire Ex

A second chance enemies to lovers romance

Annie Ireland

Join Annie's newsletter

Click the QR code to join Annie's newsletter.

Copyright © 2024 by Annie Ireland

Published by Leather & Lace Publishing

All rights reserved.

No part of this book may be reproduced in any form or by any electronic or mechanical means, including information storage and retrieval systems, without written permission from the author, except for the use of brief quotations in a book review.

Created with Vellum

Chapter 1

Theodore

The sound of the door opening distracts me for a moment.

The intruder pokes a head in first.

I lift a hand to stop Miss Jones from saying anything further.

Schooling my face from expressing surprise at the first sight of her after so many years, I lean back on my chair.

"Miss Jones, leave us."

Miss Jones nods, grabs a couple of files, and hurries away.

I note the surprise in her eyes with amusement. Surely, she can't be surprised to see me here. Nervous maybe.

"Ray," I comment, the name feeling strange in my mouth.

How long has it been? Ten years?

My eyes roam over her. Dressed in an impeccable scoop-neck knee-length green dress, she looks prim and proper, unlike the carefree and jovial girl in college.

"It's Raya, Mr. Caddel."

I smirk at her attempt at forced formality.

I stretch forth a hand. "Please, have a seat."

Leaning forward, I rest my elbows on the desk. I study Raya's profile, noting with pride how age has done little to nothing to her appearance. She's still as gorgeous as ever, and of course, ever the smart mouth.

Annie Ireland

"What brings you here?"

Did she get wind of my plans?

Hesitantly, she perches on a seat across from me, her purse clutched tightly.

"Thank you so much, Mr. Caddel. I'm sorry for barging in without an appointment. I feared you'd turn me away, and when I didn't see the secretary, I took the opportunity to sneak in."

I watch her ramble on without really listening. "Why are you here?"

She swallows.

"Look at me, Raya. Relax, okay?"

Her cheeks turn red. "Okay."

"It's a shame Miss Jones wasn't at her desk when you arrived because I certainly would've turned you away. But that's not the point. Tell me what you want."

She breaks her gaze to study her fingers. "I need your help."

"Yes?"

She clears her throat, training her eyes on me again. "It's about my father's company."

I nod. "I heard about the great King's passing. My sincere condolences." And I meant it.

A painful look fleets through her face, and then she smiles.

"Thank you. You must know the company's state if you heard about my Dad."

"I'm sorry."

She runs a finger through her hair. "Don't be. I'm here to solicit your help getting the King back on its feet."

I fold my arms over my chest.

"Will you help me?" she asks.

I shrug. "How about I buy it from you instead, save you the stress?"

"I don't need to be saved."

"Yeah? Typical Raya."

Her eyes harden. "What's that supposed to mean?"

I ignore the sharpness of her voice and pick up the intercom.

Chapter 1

"What are you doing?"

"I'm calling for coffee. I think we'll both need it."

Her brows furrow. "I'm perfectly fine, Theo."

I chuckle. "Oh, we're back to Theo now."

She snorts. "Stop making it more difficult than it already is, please."

I drop the intercom with a thud.

"Why don't you start by telling me why you broke up with me, Raya?"

She shakes her head. "Please, Theo, let's forget about the past—"

"I haven't."

"You should. It's been so long ago."

"Was it someone else?"

Over the years, I haven't been able to ignore the possibility that I wasn't enough for her.

She'd left without a goodbye, not a word. And now, out of nowhere, she suddenly shows up, asking for help.

"Was it someone else?" I press again when she doesn't answer. "Burt from chemistry?"

"No."

"Why? Weren't you two like the power couple of chemistry?"

"Burt was nothing but a study partner. Why are we even talking about this?"

I ignore her frustration, concluding, "Then I just wasn't good enough for you."

Ray looks hurt. "I left because things were complicated, not because of someone else."

I raise an eyebrow. "Complicated? Like solving a 'quantum physics equation' complicated, or 'I couldn't decide between pizza toppings' complicated?"

She sighs, clearly annoyed. "More like 'life decisions' complicated. And your sarcastic comments aren't helping."

"Oh, forgive me for not grasping the depth of your existential crisis. I thought your life decisions were choosing between Netflix shows."

Annie Ireland

"It's not that simple. Can we focus on the current issue? I need your help."

"Ah, the classic move. Leave without a word, return needing urgent assistance. You're really nailing this 'damsel in distress' routine."

Her frustration grows. "This is serious, okay? I wouldn't be here if I didn't have to be."

I lean in, pretending to be serious, then say. "Did dear Burt fail you in helping with serious matters?"

"For the last time, Burt is not the issue here! Can we just get past this?"

"Well, if Burt's not the problem, then it must be my inadequacy. Classic unresolved issues, Ray." I wiggle my eyebrows.

She looks exasperated. "Can you please be serious for once in your life?"

"Serious? Me?" I study her momentarily, contemplating whether to bother her further or ultimately make her explode. I go for the former. For now. "Fine, let's tackle your 'complicated' life problems. What would you like me to do for you?"

Ray hesitates, finally admitting, "I need funding for King's. And, I guess, some guidance."

I lean back, a sly grin forming. "Funding and guidance, you say? Easy. You know I've always been a generous soul. It's why you're here, aren't you? But then, you must also know I don't do free favors."

"What do you mean?"

"I mean, I'll consider helping you under one condition."

She eyes me suspiciously. "What condition?"

"You become my nanny," I declare, surprised by the absurdity of my own suggestion. "Live in my house, make me sandwiches, and provide stellar life advice since, you know, you have so much experience dealing with it. Deal?"

Ray's jaw drops. "Your nanny? Are you serious?"

"Absolutely," I reply with a straight face.

"Theo, can we be reasonable here, please?"

Chapter 1

"This is my office, and I do whatever I want. If you disagree with my condition, the door is open. I never called you here anyway."

If looks could kill, my battered body would probably be rotting in a rice farm in the middle of nowhere right now. Ray is losing her patience, giving me that same look she started to give me the five months that preceded our breakup. That's how I know she's about to break.

"Come on, run. It's basically your cardio, right?" I sneer.

I expect Ray to flip me off and slam my doorstep so hard that it'll fly out of its hinges. But this woman is full of surprises. After about five minutes of serious thinking, she squares her shoulders, "Fine, I'll be your nanny. But you better be ready to pay for humiliating me this way."

And, just like that, my little revenge hiatus takes a surprising turn.

Chapter 2

Raya

I want to kill Theodore Caddel.

Right from the minute I walked into the office and saw him sitting behind that giant leather chair, indicating he's the top dog here, I knew I was making a big mistake. Yet, flustered and taken aback by his transformed, mature look—quite the contrast to the Theodore I once knew—I couldn't bring myself to turn back.

Seizing a minute of his surprise on seeing me, I check out his outfit, or at least, the part of it I can see—a sharp, white shirt that fits him just right on his tall, lean frame. His black hair is neatly combed, and those ridiculously long eyelashes are as prominent as ever. I always tell myself that his thick brows are an overkill, but annoyingly, they work on his face.

Everyone knows Theodore Caddel is breathtakingly gorgeous. Even people who are blind could tell from his voice, and seeing him this formally dressed was a little too much confirmation for my liking.

Maybe he's different from the jerk he used to be, too, I presume, only to realize I'm an eternal optimist for thinking that way when he asked me to be his nanny.

Typical Theodore, treating everyone like toys.

And there's no other explanation other than unreasonableness for why I'm now nodding to his crazy deal in exchange for help.

Chapter 2

Theodore is really enjoying this, and, being the classic jerk he is, he takes it up a notch.

"You know what? I changed my mind," he says, leaning back into his seat. I wonder if I can shove him into the glass wall behind him and get away with it. "You'll also be my fake fiancè."

"After the first deal, I won't say I'm surprised."

"What's that supposed to mean?"

"It means you're still as predictable as ever, Theodore."

He raises an eyebrow, smirking. "Predictable? Please. I beg to differ. I'm full of surprises."

I laugh sarcastically. "Yeah, surprise me by not being selfish for once."

His smirk widens. "Selfish? I'm offering you the chance of a lifetime."

I can't help but roll my eyes. "A chance to play your fake fiancée? How could I resist?"

His tone turns sly, "Well, considering the alternative is dealing with your company's problems on your own, I'd say it's a pretty sweet deal."

I shoot him a look, my annoyance thinly veiled. "You really know how to make a girl feel special, Theodore. You're not that different from who you used to be."

"And who did I used to be?"

"The rich, spoiled, carefree boy who had the world handed to him on a silver platter," I reply, deciding to be brutally honest. I start to rant without pausing to take a breath. "I, on the other hand, needed to focus on building a future because I had a future to build. I broke up with you because your personality was unbearable.

I needed someone serious, not a constant distraction from my goals and responsibilities. I was a different version of myself with you. I was partying every weekend, ending up in detention every blessed day, getting into trouble with my Dad, failing my exams! And for what? For you, who didn't even understand the value of the life you had? And guess what, Theodore? You're still that immature, self-absorbed guy I walked away from."

By the time I'm done, Theodore's face is tight, and his fists clench on the table like he's about to explode. It's suddenly so quiet in here. Too quiet. I sense trouble brewing. My big mouth has landed me in a fix once again. Knowing Theodore, there's no way he's letting this go, so I may as well leave with my dignity still intact.

Feeling the weight of his stern gaze, I grab my bag, planning to exit quickly. But right as I reach the door, Theodore's voice stops me.

"Do we have a deal?" He asks quietly.

I turn back, "I can't change your mind, can I?"

Theodore doesn't answer.

"Is there something you want to gain from this? You want to punish me?" I press on.

He leans forward, a steely look in his eyes. "It's simple, really. Take my offer, or kiss your Dad's company goodbye."

I hesitate, hating myself for getting myself into this. But I'm desperate. Too desperate to save King's. After a moment of intense contemplation, I sigh and reluctantly agree. "Fine, Theodore. We have a deal."

Pleased, Theodore leans back into his seat. "I'll draw up a contract after ...," He glances at his calendar. "After Vicky's wedding this Thursday."

"Tell her congratulations."

"Oh, she hates you. Nobody breaks a Caddel's heart and gets away with it, especially when it's Vicky's favorite cousin."

That stings, but I shrug indifferently, "Fair enough."

"So, the contract will be drawn after the wedding. But I must warn you. This will be done on my terms, Raya. My terms."

I'm so going to regret this, but I shrug again. "Whatever."

Chapter 3

Theodore

Vicky's spring wedding theme reminds me just how much I hate the season, and the ceremony itself reminds me why I should never attend family gatherings alone.

My family began to attack right after the church service after they caught me trying to slip away.

"So, Theodore, when's the big day? Or are you planning to set a record for the world's most eligible bachelor?"

Focus on your third divorce in two years. I want to retort, but Uncle Bob's the bride's favorite Uncle, so I keep that to myself.

"Seriously, Ted, do you like men? This is a safe space, you know," Aunt Winifred, the ringleader of these family bullies, asks.

Clearly, being a world-class billionaire means nothing to these people. They will bully you into getting what they want, be it a wedding or a child.

"Maybe you should consider a career change and start a YouTube channel, 'Life Lessons from the Perpetual Bachelor.' I'm sure it would be a hit," Aunty Carol says and bursts out laughing, expecting others to laugh at her dry joke. No one does.

"I mean, who needs a wedding when you can have weekly pizza nights and Netflix marathons, right, Theodore?"

Annie Ireland

"I don't have such time on my hands, Susan," I answer Susan, a distant part of the family who's the only one in my age group. "Unlike some people, I'm not contesting for the position of the laziest Caddel."

Dad, with a smirk, adds, "Be nice to Susan. She's only looking out for you like the rest of us. She isn't the one who promised to bring someone home by my sixtieth birthday and failed. Anyway, time's ticking for sixty-fifth. Get ready."

I roll my eyes. Like he hasn't been ringing that in my ears every day in the past year. Thankfully, my phone rings at that moment. It's Vicky asking if I can pick up the emergency cake for the reception since the first got ruined. In other words, it's an emergency I'm more than glad to use to get out of there, even if it costs me more time and energy than I wanted to spend at the wedding.

The reception party starts a little while later. The couple, Vicky and Brad, stand under a simple arch covered in daisies and tulips. The numerous tables are dressed in soft pastels decorated with small bouquets of fresh blooms. Guests sit on white chairs, and a gentle breeze plays with the colorful ribbons.

It's a bit too colorful for my taste, but honestly, everything looks nice. The only problem is those little signs on each chair pushing everyone to trust Evergreen Bridals for their big days.

The foot traffic is quite tight. My youngest cousin, Savannah, the bride's sister, is spying on the guests and sharing where the attractive guys are hanging out. Lily, Vicky's best friend, is now determinedly trying to get a groomsman's phone number after spending the last hour trying to flirt with me. Mom is occupied telling little Cami not to eat the flowers.

All the men at the party have somehow disappeared. Dad is laughing his insides out at some dry jokes with Vicky's Dad and some business associates. Mickey and Fred are running errands, and Ethan is nowhere to be found.

My tuxedo feels like it's shrinking with every tick of the clock. Eventually, Ethan finds me, and as he takes a deep breath, then lets it out slowly, I

Chapter 3

catch him swearing under his breath. He doesn't need to glance at me to sense something's off.

He glances up at me, waiting. "Still selling drugs?"

I clench my teeth. "You know I never did."

"Your father begs to differ. And I don't blame him. You were quite the troublemaker in High school, and you look the part right now."

"Seriously, what's wrong with all of you? I wasn't even that bad!"

"Did someone else talk about this? Is that why you look like shooting everyone here?"

"I hate weddings."

"But you're here anyway, so it's not why you're this worked up. Whatever it is, just say it."

I glare at Ethan but still narrate the ordeal between me and Raya, carefully reiterating that she's the ex I used to tell him about and how I should have kicked her out immediately. Ethan's brows furrowed in confusion after every sentence, and then he chuckled. I swear I am not a violent man, but at the sight of his mocking smile, the urge to drown him in my champagne is nearly irresistible.

Finally, he says, "What on earth were you thinking? Are you trying to start a rom-com?"

"It's a strategic arrangement. What the fuck is a rom-com? Sounds like something I want to stay away from."

"Well, clearly you're not. And what do you mean, strategic arrangement? Dude, I can practically see the movie poster."

"It's just a way to get what I need. Nothing more."

"Surely this is not about Aunty Winifred harassing you for a wife?" Ethan asks, studying me a little too intently. "And don't say yes because I know you don't care about all these people's opinions."

"Fuck you, man."

Ethan laughs. "You know, denial is not just a river in Egypt. Admit it, you still have feelings for her."

"No way. It's purely a business arrangement," I answer.

"Uh-huh, business. Tell me more about the logic behind this cutting-edge business strategy of making your ex-nanny-fiancée."

It's getting frustrating having to think about the absurdity of my actions. And knowing Ethan, he won't stop pointing it out. I answer, "Look, she needed my help, and I didn't want to give it out that easily. Stop exaggerating. It's just a temporary thing."

"Temporary until you realize you can't resist her charm. Have you forgotten how hard you fell and how messed up you were after the breakup? Dude, you sang 'Un-Break My Heart' in the shower for a month straight. I thought you were auditioning for a dramatic musical."

I narrow my eyes at Ethan, cringing at the memory, "Don't you dare breathe a word of that to anyone."

He chuckles, "Your secret's safe, man. For now."

I glance at my watch. "I've been here for too long. The flowers are starting to sicken me. Tell Vicky I was the last person to leave this venue."

"You do know she'll kill you for letting Raya back into your life, don't you?"

"That's if she finds out."

Ethan clicks his tongue, shaking his head, "Trust me, you're the leading man in your love story. I'll be here to tell you I told you so because, trust me, this woman has always had—and still has—a special kind of power over you, no matter how hard you deny it."

"Enough with the rom-com nonsense. I'm out of here."

I leave the venue and enter my waiting Bentley Mulsanne, more unsettled than ever. I don't know if I'm just annoyed at myself or Ethan for giving me a reason to be annoyed at myself. Raya? Power over me? I scoff.

My phone rings in my pocket, and I pull it out. Speak of the devil.

"Is the contract ready?" Raya's tired voice asks. What has she been doing?

"No, but meet me at Stars and Stripes in thirty."

"Why?"

"It's part of the process," Is all I say and hang up.

My heartbeat quickens at the sight of Raya standing near the mall

Chapter 3

entrance. Today, she's wearing a blue wraparound dress paired with matching heels, her hair elegantly arranged atop her head, and oversized sunglasses resting delicately on the bridge of her nose.

I pause for a moment and take her in. She looks older and more put together. More beautiful. Her curves are prominent, and her skin is glowing under the sun. One wouldn't even expect that a woman like her is going through a crisis. It's one of the things that attracted me to her in the first place.

As I park and hand the car to the valet, I see a few men turning their heads to have a second look at Raya. I quickly stop myself from feeling a familiar irritation when she gets too much attention from men but fails. A little bit of the anger has seeped in.

Raya looks up and straightens when she notices me approaching.

"Hi," she says tightly as the security man holds the door open for us. "Where are we going?"

"To play football," I answer sarcastically as we enter the air-conditioned store. The manager gets tense and hurries over when he sees me, wearing a nervous smile. He's an older guy, and his graying hair and well-pressed suit give me a neat outlook. If he weren't so jittery, he'd match the fancy vibe of this store.

"Mr. Caddel," he says, then turns to Raya wide-eyed. "Miss King." His eyes check out Raya's body like guys always do.

"It's an honor meeting you, Miss King. I'm Greg, and I'm here to help you today."

I get all tense and grab Raya's shoulder. I notice her looking at me in surprise, but I'm too focused on the store manager, staring at him with barely concealed annoyance. "We'll ask for help when we need it," I tell him, not bothering to sound nice.

I steer Raya towards the glass display counters, feeling tense.

"What's wrong with you?" she asks once we're out of earshot.

I let go of her and shake my head. "He's not professional. The way he looked at you just now? What was that?"

"I believe it's him offering us good customer service."

Annie Ireland

"More like eye service," I mutter, annoyed.

She shoots me a sarcastic look. "You're overreacting, as usual."

I huff, "I'm not overreacting. It's just weird. And the way he said 'Miss King' like he's auditioning for a movie."

"He's being polite. You could learn a thing or two about manners."

I roll my eyes, "I've got plenty of manners, thank you very much."

"What are we even doing here?" She asks, throwing her hands in frustration.

I roll my eyes and turn to look at the jewelry on display. My eyes move over the engagement rings. The idea of me getting engaged for real seems really hard to believe. I can't imagine wanting to marry anyone and spending the rest of my life with them.

"Are we here to buy engagement rings?" Raya asks, but I ignore her.

There's one ring that catches my eye. I know it'll be perfect, but I quickly get tired of the glitters. My gaze settles on a classic diamond. "How about something like that?"

"Seriously, what are you doing?"

I call Greg over, and he hands the ring to me before pointing to the mirror behind me. I take Raya's hand and slip it on, wanting to check its appearance, and she flinches slightly.

"It's a perfect fit," I tell her.

I shake my head. "Oh no, I can't. This is too expensive for—"

I quickly cut her off. "Bah, bah, bah. What are you doing?"

Raya looks at Greg, who's beaming.

"We'll call you again," I say, and he scrambles off immediately.

"It's a fake engagement. What the hell are you doing?"

"My terms, remember?" I smirk, enjoying the control I have.

Raya's eyes narrow, "Don't push it, Theodore. This is supposed to be a business deal."

I lean in, "But my terms include some creative freedom. I can even kiss you if I want."

Her warning is clear, "Don't you dare."

It is an invitation I can't resist. Cupping her face, I lean in and press

Chapter 3

my lips to hers. When she gasps, I seize the moment, indulging in a deep, passionate, wet kiss. No formalities. It's been ages since we kissed. Years. Some part of me wants to remind her that we used to be incredible together.

She murmurs my name in the sexiest, softest whisper and digs her fingers into my biceps, trying to get closer. Closer suits me just fine, and I let myself explore, letting my hands wander over her exquisite body. I don't care that we are in public. All that's in my head is how much I've missed this.

She moans into the kiss but gently pulls back. Breathing heavily, she shakes her head. "What... What are you doing?"

"You like it?" I lean in for another kiss, but she places a hand on my chest.

"We're in public," she groans, making no effort to push me away.

"Are you saying you want to go back to my place?"

Raya looks at me sharply, pressing her hands flat against my chest and giving me a strong push.

Despite her effort, I remain steady, holding onto her.

Frustrated, she makes a sound of irritation and shoves me again. "Let me go."

I raise my hands, letting go.

She steps back, crossing her arms after she straightens her dress. "We shouldn't do that again."

"Why not? Seemed to me like you enjoyed it."

She presses me with a glare. "Any form of intimacy is off-limits. I won't give you my body. Those are my terms."

I chuckle, closing the distance between us. "Oh, it's on your terms until I decide otherwise. Remember, my terms, my rules."

Chapter 4

Raya

Packing is harder than I thought. Fitting my entire life into a few boxes isn't easy. I don't have a lot, just some basic stuff I bought when I came back to the country.

These things aren't fancy, but I care about them. They've been good to me. Now, I have to get rid of most of them and give them away to people who won't get why they mean something to me.

Kaylee, my best friend, came over last night to help me. It took more than a couple of hours to get her to understand why I was making this decision. Even then, she'd throw in questions occasionally, and I'd have to explain all over again.

Today, she's not letting me off the hook so easily.

"So, you're sure nothing's going on with you and that Greek God outside?" Kaylee asks, folding my clothes into a duffel bag.

"Nothing, Kaylee. Forget his looks. He's a jerk."

"How can I forget his looks? That man's fineeeee with a capital F, and he knows it," She drawls on the 'fine' dramatically. I roll my eyes.

. . .

Chapter 4

"If I ever have the chance to work as his personal assistant, I'd get extra personal with him," She winks suggestively, making me laugh.

"Trust me, he's not all that. You'd hate him more than I do."

She raises an eyebrow, clearly not buying it. "Raya, I've known you forever. You can't fool me. This," she gestures at all my scattered stuff. "Can't just be an act. He even came to pick you up himself. Didn't you say he had a company to run?"

"Come on, Kaylee. I've told you a zillion times that it's all an act. He's not planning anything, and he definitely doesn't like me," I say, doubting my own words. Two days ago, I wouldn't have questioned that Theo hated me at all. But after that kiss at the jewelry store...

I can't help but think about it, how it made me feel all kinds of things from my heart to between my legs. I blush, remembering it like it just happened.

Kaylee leans forward, studying me intently. "You're sure about that?"

"Positive. It's just a business deal, nothing more," I insist, avoiding eye contact. "Keep packing. He'll break this door down anytime soon."

But instead of packing, Kaylee's eyes narrow even further. "Alright, spill the tea. What happened?"

I hesitate, then sigh. How does she always sniff out my secrets without even trying? I shoot her an accusatory look, but I only get flustered by her looks. She's the definition of gamine and gorgeous with her strawberry blond hair in place and twinkling brown eyes that capture even the least obvious things.

"Okay, fine. Well, um, I went to a jewelry store yesterday to pick out our fake engagement rings."

Her eyes widen in surprise. "You didn't tell me about that!"

I shrug sheepishly. "It was a last-minute thing. Anyway, while we were there, Theodore kissed me."

Kaylee nearly chokes. "He did what? And you didn't tell me immediately?"

Annie Ireland

"I didn't know how to bring it up!" I defend myself. "And it's not like it meant anything. It's just part of the act."

She leans back, processing the information. "So, he kissed you. That's a bold move for a fake engagement."

"I know, right? But it doesn't mean anything. It was just to make our engagement look convincing," I explain, trying to convince myself more.

"Raya, you've got to be careful. This sounds like he's still into you."

I roll my eyes. "Kaylee, please. He's not. If anything, Theodore Caddel hates my guts for breaking up with him. Besides, we're adults, and we're just doing this for Dad's company. Nothing more."

She sighs, clearly unconvinced. "Just promise me you'll be cautious. I don't want to see you getting hurt."

"I've got everything under control, but I promise to be careful," I assure her, but deep down, a lingering doubt dances in the corners of my mind. I reach into my handbag and pull out the fake engagement ring. "See? It's just a prop."

Kaylee takes the ring from me and inspects it, her eyes narrowing again. "It looks real. And it's pretty convincing. Are you sure this is just for show?"

"Trust me."

She sighs, reluctantly accepting my explanation. "I guess you do have to do anything it takes to save King's. I admire your resilience, girl, but if things start getting too complicated, promise me you'll talk to me about it. No more secrets, okay?"

"No more secrets. I promise," I say, nodding.

"What should I do with this?" Kaylee asks, handing me a blender from Tracey, my neighbor.

Feeling oddly sentimental over the blender, I let out a sigh and put it in the throw-out box. My heart isn't in any of this, my mind repeatedly replaying the part when I walked into Theodore's office. A part of me, the conditioned part of me, wants to give him a giant middle finger and reclaim my pride. My other part is helpless, knowing I have nowhere else to go for help.

Chapter 4

Kaylee finished her part of the work and left, promising to bring me the necessary toiletries by tomorrow morning.

As I hitch an awkward ride in Theodore's car, I rethink my actions. I should be out getting blackout drunk to forget my problems instead of allowing this man to trample all over my pride, which is making me feel worse.

I feel foolish and emotionally drained, yet I know the worst is yet to come.

* * *

This morning, I don't step out of my room until I'm certain Theodore has left. It's been two days since I moved in, and we've only spoken once to schedule a time for signing the contract.

It's the best strategy to keep the cunning man from breaking through my defenses, preventing me from thinking about our kiss more than I want to. I gather my hair into a tight knot, snatch my purse, and leave the room. I reach the bottom of the stairs just as the doorbell rings.

Kaylee.

"Should I be glad or worried that you two haven't killed each other yet?" Kaycee asks, pulling me in for a hug. I take the bag from her and lead her in.

"Wow, this place is huge!"

Kaylee is right. Theodore's place is just like I imagined. It's huge, with the living room twice the size of my apartment. There's a luxurious, lavishly furnished seating area, all expensive black couches, and soft white cushions. There's also a fancy coffee table adorned with large, glossy books, a workspace featuring the latest iMac model, and a massive plasma screen TV mounted on the wall.

"Is he some kind of neat freak?"

"Always has been."

"Oh, my. Are we talking alphabetized bookshelves and color-coded sock drawers?"

"More like a vacuum lines in the carpet kind of guy. Everything has its designated spot."

"He'd explode when he discovers your ... um, chaotic organizational methods. It would be best if you kept doing whatever it is you did to stop yourself from killing him. I'd advise he does the same, too."

"We're mostly ignoring each other, and that's helping me stay out of jail." I chuckle and unzip the bag to check the things Kaylee brought. They are intact: undies, clothes, handbags, and...

"What's this?" I ask, taking out an unopened sachet of pills from the box. The pills look oddly familiar, and I pray it isn't what I think it is.

"Birth control pills."

Yep, the pills are frustratingly precisely what I think they are. "I reckoned you would need them for...you know?"

"I'm not planning to have sex with this guy!" I cry in frustration.

"It's a precaution. You never can tell what happens when you're in the vicinity of such sexiness, especially with someone you've had sex with. How were his oral skills?"

I think I just died a little.

As if on cue, Theodore chooses that moment to walk through the kitchen door. I recoil in embarrassment and put the pills away, but Theodore's raised eyebrow tells me he saw it. Thankfully, he doesn't seem to have recognized it.

"Y... you're in?" I stammer.

"You seem disappointed," Theo says dully, completely ignoring Kaylee before sauntering up the stairs.

Ugh, moody.

The man is moody this morning for reasons I do not know, but I don't bother myself with that. There are other essential things I need to focus on. For example, getting through my day without clashing with Theodore and getting some work done on King's company—hopefully with his help.

Kaylee hung around till later that morning and left after she got an emergency work call, which meant I had to start my day, too. The bath-

Chapter 4

room is all hot and steamy. I undress and step into the water pouring from the high-end shower. It soothes my skin in a welcoming torrent, making me soak in it longer than intended.

I step out of the shower, using one towel for my hair, Carmen Miranda style, and the other to quickly dry myself. Rummaging through the bag Kaylee brought, I discover not only the pills and toiletries but also exquisite lingerie in matching pale blue lace that leaves nothing to the imagination. I blush furiously, wondering what must have been going through my best friend's mind.

Thinking it won't hurt to try them off, I take the towel off my body and slip the panties on. The unexpected touch of luxury makes me smile, and I twirl in the mirror, giggling like a child.

I sit down, stretch out my legs, and tug the fabric down over my ass.

And, of course, that's when Theodore opens the door.

"Hey, where have you—" The words hang heavy when he walks in on me because I don't move—frozen, even though I am entirely off balance.

Theodore impulsively rushes to me and steadies me with his hands on my hips, and I swallow down my quickly rising hysteria.

He is staring innocently. Except I know Theodore, and there isn't much innocence to him. There never has been. His strong hands hold me in place, and when his eyes slowly tear away from my face and down my body, it feels like the air is charged with electricity.

He wants me. I can see it in his eyes.

I hold my breath, slowly moving away from him, but his muscles respond like a big cat, arms pinning me in place. One hand firmly on my shoulders, the other possessively sliding down and grabbing my backside. His breathing stays steady, like a tortoise, yet he's more like a sneaky cheetah. His serious gaze is fixed on me.

"Sorry," I mumble, attempting to free myself, but he tightens his grip, still not smiling.

Theodore's eyes grow heavy. "What are you doing to me, Raya?"

There is just something about the way he says my name. He is trying to act unaffected, but his veneer is cracking. The tightrope we have been walking on all day is fraying. One thread snapping at a time.

It is then I realize I want the last thread to snap.

Damn the consequences. I've been unintentionally celibate for too long to care. Besides, he wants this, too.

Maybe that is why I grab his face and crash my lips to his.

Chapter 5

Theodore

I'm about to go crazy, but I don't feel bad about it. All I can feel is Raya's lips on mine as she kisses me senselessly and her soft, warm skin pressing against my body.

What started as a soft, gentle kiss grows into something none of us can control, leading us to the bed.

Pausing to steady myself, I flip us so my firm body blankets hers. My mouth glides across her cheek, a deliberate path towards her lips, providing ample opportunity for her to stop me from doing what I'm about to do to her. No coherent words escape from her lips. Instead, her body resounds with a silent, "Yes, yes, yes, Theodore." she breathes.

"You shouldn't have been playing around naked like that."

"No, I…"

I turn my head, and my lips graze the inside of her arm. It dawns on me that both her arms are tightly wrapped around me—she's holding on to me. I playfully nip the skin I just kissed, sensing her response.

"Okay, yes," she admits. "But I didn't mean for you to see."

Lowering my head, I guide my mouth along her jaw, down her throat, and against the hollow of her collarbone. "I've been crazy wondering what you were always up to here," I murmur.

I want her to focus on my words, but she shivers shivers through her entire body in response to me.

"Please," she whispers, holding onto me to prevent any escape—like I plan to. She shuts her eyes. "Please, no small talk. Don't ... Don't toy with me."

I freeze above her. "Is that what you think I'm doing?"

My warm breath against her skin, I can't resist tasting, igniting a fiery sensation within me. Our gaze meets, her eyes dark and heated. Sliding a hand down her leg, I pull it up around my hip, grinding into her. I'm hard, my mouth warm, firm, and perfect—both familiar and entirely new and exciting.

"Does that feel like I'm playing a game, Raya?"

You'll regret it later, my brain reminds me.

In the battle between my overpowering hormones and dwindling brain cells, Raya's body is irresistibly pressed against me, and it's clear her body is emerging victorious. "Raya—"

My hand caresses her cheek, fingers weaving into her hair at the back of her neck. Tilting her head up, I wait until our eyes meet, the tension crackling in the air.

"Are we going to stop?" I ask, my voice thrillingly strained, sending another shiver up her spine.

"No," she whispers.

Perfect.

I hold her gaze, grappling with my inner battle. Finally, I lean forward, brushing my lips to hers. Her low moan grants me the access I crave, and I deepen the kiss, my tongue stroking hers. She squirms, trying to get closer. Rolling over her, I never break the kiss as I cup the back of her head, my thumbs stroking her throat. Her hands slide beneath my shirt, feeling the carefully leashed power beneath my skin. I want to unleash that power on her more than I want my next breath.

Throughout all this time, over the years, the way she made me feel has never escaped my memory. I wonder, has she made other men feel this

Chapter 5

same way? Does my touch linger in her memory as much as hers does in mine?

I can't recall the last time I lost myself in passion and desire. There have been a few women after Raya, and it's been pleasant... but I crave more than just pleasant. I yearn to completely let go, and I know Raya has the power to make me do that.

My hands move south, savoring the best buns I've ever had the pleasure of gripping. When she draws me closer, my mouth descends on hers—hungry, edgy, and demanding. Indeed, one kiss can't be everything, but this one is.

And I adore it. I thrive on it.

She looks stunning in the flickering light, her chest rising and falling quickly as her breath speeds up. I run my hands up her body, my thumbs grazing her tight nipples. She responds, arching into my touch. Turning my face, I kiss the sensitive skin behind her knee, aware of her reaction. Tracing the dip with my tongue, I repeat the process on her other leg, grinning as I feel her muscles tighten.

Slowly, I lick, kiss, and nibble my way up her thighs, alternating between the two, using my fingers to pinch and squeeze.

As I get closer, her soft whimpers grow louder, my thumbs resting on each side. Delicately, I separate her lips and bring my mouth close, flattening my tongue and sliding it over her sensitive area.

She arches from the bed, her body tense. Using my mouth, I alternate between extended, forceful strokes and gentle flicks of my tongue. I insert one finger, then two, coordinating their movements to push her to the brink before easing off, aiming to prolong her pleasure.

Gripping the back of my neck, her fingers are restless, tugging at my hair. She moans my name, craving more, pleading with me. Her arousal tightens around my fingers, and my desire intensifies, eager to feel her warmth. I quicken my movements, providing what she desires, using my fingers to pleasure her swiftly and focusing on her sensitive area until her body shudders, overwhelmed with ecstasy, as she reaches a powerful climax.

She emits a soft, low sound and brings my forehead to hers. "Condom."

My mind goes blank. "Oh my God."

Did I genuinely almost forget protection?

"You better have a condom. Tell me you have a condom!"

"I have a condom." Standing, I confidently walk to my bedroom, completely nude, and return quickly.

"Okay," she says with a sigh of relief.

I open the foil. She takes the condom from me, unrolling it onto me as I observe. By the time it's on, I'm already inside her.

I enter her body with a strong, urgent thrust that makes both of us gasp with pleasure. I move with long, powerful strokes, holding onto her hips, keeping her close as I make her mine. Her sounds encourage me, her soft moans and pleas fueling my desire. She's hot and wet, gripping me intensely. I adjust my angle, leaning over her, supporting myself with one hand as I bring her mouth up to meet mine with the other.

Our tongues move together, matching the rhythm of our bodies. Raya shivers as I slide my hand over the curve of her ass, pulling her closer. I ease my movements, slowing down, my thrusts becoming unhurried. I sway my hips, hitting the spot she craves. I love her the way I know she wants.

She gasps as I change the angle, letting me go even deeper. I moan. The sensations are overwhelming. Tonight, she's everywhere, stirring up emotions and making my body long for her.

"Come for me, darling. I won't hold on much more, and I want you to come first," I plead. I put my hand between us, gently touching her clit the way she enjoys. "Please."

She shouts, holding onto my shoulders, reaching her climax. Her short nails dig into my skin as she arches and moves. Her muscles tighten and release around me, triggering my orgasm. It feels like hot liquid fire, electrifying my nerves. I tense, and I explode, immersed in the pleasure that I only feel with Raya.

Bliss.

Chapter 5

It was always about the physical with other women, but I can't deny that this is different. It isn't just about the physical; there's a deep emotional connection that we've always shared.

I bury my face in her neck, riding out waves of bliss. Words tumble from my mouth, saying her name repeatedly until I'm spent. I collapse into her, only feeling her softness and warmth.

Moments go by, and I gently roll us to the side, not wanting to let go but realizing I need to ease my weight off. I nestle into her tousled hair, which I had tangled with my hands.

I kiss her neck, the same one I licked and nibbled in my excitement. I caress her back, the skin damp and warm from our connection. I keep her close until our trembling stops, and we can talk again.

"That was amazing," is all I can muster, feeling fatigue wash over me.

Beside me, I see Raya is also spent. Her eyes close, and she drifts off to sleep in no time. I lie there, thinking about what just happened, and it hits me – Ethan was right. Raya still has this kind of power over me beyond just the physical.

As she falls deeper, I realize it's more than I thought. It's not just about what happened between us tonight; it's like she has this magnetic pull on me, even after all this time.

Carefully slipping away from her, so I don't wake her up, I take a moment to look at her in the soft light. The room is quiet, and she seems so peaceful.

Slipping out, I'm questioning if I can break free from the hold she has on me or if, deep down, I'm still caught up in the emotions she brings out in me.

I guess time will tell.

* * *

I wake up to the unmistakable scent of something about to burn seriously. The thick smell wafts into the bedroom, and for a moment, I'm disoriented. I told the housekeeper to take the week off, so who could cook or try to burn my house down?

Rubbing the sleep from my eyes, I make my way to the kitchen only to see Raya at the stove, focused on taming what appears to be a pancake that is bent on flipping itself right out of the pan.

"You're up," she says with a grin, her attention briefly shifting from the pancakes.

I chuckle, still half-asleep. "Yeah, I am. What's going on here?"

She shrugs, flushing when the pancake eventually flies out of the pan and onto the marble countertop. "Thought I'd make breakfast."

I raise an eyebrow, skeptical but amused. "And how's that going?" My eyes roam over the mess that was once my kitchen. Pots and pans are everywhere, and there's flour and God-knows-what everywhere. It's like a breakfast explosion happened here. I look at Raya, and she's proudly holding up the slightly crispy pancake with an oven mitt like a trophy.

"It formed!" She sounds genuinely happy and even makes a cute jump. I chuckle.

"I guess you're improving. Because the last time you tried making breakfast, we ended up with burnt toast and scrambled eggs that could've doubled as rubber balls."

"I told you they were just extra crispy!" She shoots me a glare, and I raise my hand in mock surrender.

"Okay, okay. Extra crispy, just how your Mom and everyone else liked it."

She grimaces, dropping the pancake on a nearby plate. "Okay, maybe I've been stabbing my cooking tutorials."

I lean against the kitchen counter and fold my arms. "Well, this was a pleasant wake-up call. I'm sorry it didn't turn out well."

"I'll clean up," Raya says dejectedly.

"Just leave it," I tell her.

She glances at me, giving me a confused look. "Why? I made this mess; I should clean it up. I mean, I'm the nanny, remember?"

Chapter 5

I shake my head. "Not for this morning. You've done enough, and I want you to rest."

"Since when do you care about me getting some rest?" Raya asks, raising an eyebrow.

I hesitate for a moment, not sure if I want to say what's on my mind. "Well, we did have quite the night, and I thought you might need some recovery time."

"What are—" Raya's quick clapback hangs in the air after she processes my words. She gapes, a blush working up her neck from inside her shirt's round neck.

"Yeah, "I nod knowingly. "After last night, you've earned a break." I stood upright, slowly walking into the kitchen toward her. I can see her chest heaving as her breathing quickens. "I figured you might need some time to recover because, you know, we'll be doing more of it."

I close the remaining space between us, feeling my cock grow rock hard when I sniff her. I'm dying to put her against this kitchen wall and fuck her senseless, but doing that will mean showing her just how much control she has over me. I've done that before, but it didn't turn out well. I'd been burned by her badly. Even a crawling baby can learn not to play with fire—no matter how attracted to it he is.

Raya's expression remains serious. She sets the spatula down and looks up at me, her tone measured. "Look, about last night... it was a mistake."

I feel a knot forming in my stomach. I didn't see that one coming. "What do you mean?"

She takes a breath, avoiding eye contact as she steps away from me. "I mean, what happened between us shouldn't have happened. It was a one-time thing, and it won't be happening again."

"My terms, remember?" I sneer, ignoring how my chest feels like it's been dipped in ice.

"Your terms don't give you the right to treat me like some pawn in your game," Raya says crossly.

I scoff, "You agreed to this arrangement. Don't act like you're some innocent victim here."

Her eyes narrow, "I never agreed to intimacy with you. As far as I remember, you promised a written contract that never materialized, which means the terms are still open. This is a mutual agreement, Theo. You can't unilaterally dictate terms for me any more than I can for you. It's not a chess game; it's a business arrangement. I won't allow myself to be used. This was a mistake, and I won't let it occur again."

I step closer, my tone condescending, but I don't care. "Mistake or not, you can't just change the rules whenever it suits you."

"Don't you get that this isn't about changing the rules but about realizing this isn't healthy for either of us?"

I laugh, a bitter edge to my tone. "Healthy? Spare me the moral lecture. We both know what this is about. You spread for fucking legs, had me buried inside, and urged me on. You enjoyed it just as much as I did."

"That doesn't mean it's right, and it certainly doesn't mean I'll let it continue. Let's be mature and reasonable about this."

I shake my head, dismissing her concerns. "You're being overly dramatic. We're adults; we can handle a little fun without turning it into a soap opera."

"Is that what you call it? This isn't fun, Theodore. It's a mess, and I won't let you turn it into some twisted game." Raya says through clenched teeth.

"You're always overreacting, and it's seriously starting to piss me off. We're both consenting adults. What's the harm?"

"The harm is that I won't let you toy with my body. I won't let you use me for your selfish desires."

I lean in, my tone dripping with venom. "You act like you're some saint. Let's not pretend you didn't want this as much as I did."

"Wanting something doesn't mean it's good for us. And it certainly doesn't justify your arrogant behavior."

I chuckle, unfazed. "Arrogant or not, you're here because you wanted this. Don't play the victim now."

She takes a step back, her frustration turning into resignation. "I'm

Chapter 5

done arguing with you, Theodore. This ends now. Let's just focus on being business partners for now."

But I press on, unwilling to let go of the upper hand. "Fine. Business partners it is. In that case, let's not forget your role in this house. A nanny," I press her with a gaze and add with a tone of finality, "That's all you are in here. That's why you will clean this house in preparation for my business meeting. I've noticed how disorganized you are and won't let my team come into your mess. But that's just the beginning. I want you to personally handpick the rarest flowers for the vase in the foyer and arrange them according to the color spectrum. Iron each page of my newspaper, and ensure the sunlight hits it at a perfect 45-degree angle on my study table. I need my coffee served at precisely 98 degrees Fahrenheit, not a degree more, not a degree less. Oh, and don't forget to pick up my dry cleaning, arrange my schedule, and ensure my favorite snacks are stocked. After all, that's your purpose here, isn't it, servant?"

Raya's expression tightens. Yet, she nods and keeps her composure. "I understand. I'll take care of it."

"Good." I spin on my heels and walk away, unable to ignore the hurt look on Raya's face after I strip her of her ego in spite. That face will haunt me for days to come, but I don't care.

I've had enough; I won't engage in her stupid games. It's either she wants me, or she doesn't.

Chapter 6

Raya

I hate Theodore so much.
Wiping down the last bit of coffee on the table, I picture having his stupidly gorgeous face in my hands and cleaning the entire house with it.

He's even laughing so loud with his stupid business partners right now.

Despite wanting to slap that smile off Theo's face, I'm insanely aware of his eyes following me around the living room. All that man has to do is talk, and my pulse races. Every fantasy I have involves him in some way, shape, or form. But he's an irredeemable jerk and I couldn't go there no matter how much I'd want to.

But, at least he's meeting his partners on how to help my company, even though I'm stuck on the sidelines, cleaning away invisible specks and getting more frustrated by the second.

"Listen intently, but be quiet. I'm only letting you in the room because I need you to know what's going on. Leave the discussion to me." He had strictly warned me.

I folded my arms in defiance. "I've watched Dad run this company for years. I know how to handle business discussions. I'm not a rookie."

Theo smirks, dismissive. "You might be 'watching' your Dad run the

Chapter 6

company, but you don't understand the cutthroat world of these businessmen. They'll take advantage of you at every opportunity."

"I can hold my own. I won't let anyone cheat me," I insist, but Theo brushes me off. "You're too naive. Just stay quiet and learn something for once."

Now, anytime I show the slightest interest in the ongoing discussion, Theo would shoot me a look, warning me to keep quiet. I know this is beyond wanting to protect me. It's payback for our last big fight. Unfair, right? They're talking about the business I built, and I can't even share my thoughts.

"Gentlemen," Theodore tries his third approach to convince Richard Harper, Alexander Chambers, and Evelyn Bennett. The first two were unsuccessful. "What if I propose a bold marketing strategy that will undoubtedly boost our sales? By leveraging our online presence and targeting a younger demographic, we can tap into an untapped market."

"But won't that require a significant budget increase? We need to be cautious with our spending." Evelyn counters almost immediately.

"Yes, there'll be an initial investment, but the returns far outweigh the costs. We'll see a surge in brand visibility and customer engagement."

"I'm not convinced. What about our current customer base? We can't risk alienating them with such a drastic shift," Richard says.

"We won't alienate them; we'll enhance their experience. This strategy will breathe new life into our brand. It'll appeal to both existing and potential customers."

"Look, Mr. Caddel. We appreciate the enthusiasm, but we need to assess the potential risks. The market is volatile, and a sudden shift might not play out as expected."

Theo is getting frustrated. I can tell from the way his fingers are drumming on his lap. It doesn't affect his calm demeanor, though. This man may be an asshole, but he looks hot and gorgeous, especially when he's in work mode. He's wearing a nicely tailored suit, and instead of his usual short haircut, his black hair is a bit longer, almost curly. It seems like he skipped his visit to the barber.

"I understand the concerns, but innovation comes with risks. We can't stagnate; we need to adapt to stay competitive."

"Alright, why don't you outline these methods? Let's hear your plans," Alexander says.

As they start suggesting things that could ruin everything, I can't bite my tongue any longer.

"Wait, that won't work," I blurt out. The room goes silent, and Theo shoots me this irritated, cautious look.

Evelyn raises an eyebrow. "Who are you?"

"I'm the one who started this company," I fire back. Frustration's bubbling up. "I know what works. Your idea's too risky; we need a safer approach."

Theo's jaw tightens, a clear 'shut up' in his eyes. But I don't care. My company matters more than his disapproval.

Surprisingly, Alexander nods. "She's got a point. Maybe we should play it safe."

Theo glares at me, but Alex's support boosts my confidence. I keep pushing my ideas, ignoring Theo's subtle attempts to shut me down. The meeting shifts as the partners start considering my suggestions.

Things start to look good for a while. However, a hitch in the plan stops the negotiations. The partners conclude that investing in Kings is too risky, and they unanimously decide to pass. Theodore, already upset, doesn't try to convince them further. He just gets up and accompanies them out.

When he returns, his stern expression suggests he's not thrilled with how the meeting went. I brace myself for what's coming.

"Well, that could've gone better."

"Could've if you had followed my instructions and stayed quiet." His accusation is sharp and immediate. I wince.

"I couldn't just sit there and watch. I know my family's company better than anyone."

Theo's voice rises. "This isn't about knowing your company!" He

Chapter 6

pauses, pacing to calm himself. It works. "It's about knowing how to play the politics of these meetings. You're too emotional, too impulsive."

"Emotional? Impulsive? I was defending my company!"

"And you jeopardized potential deals. Businessmen like them won't take you seriously if you don't follow the rules."

"I'm not going to let them dictate everything. I have a say in my company's future."

"You have a say, but there's a way to voice it without alienating potential partners. It's a delicate balance. Do I have to teach you every fucking thing?" He runs his hands through his hair.

Theo's words are hurtful, but I won't let it show. My voice is low. "I don't need a lecture on diplomacy. I need support and understanding."

"And that's what I'm giving you! I'm trying to save your company from your recklessness."

"My recklessness? I was there when King's was built from the ground up. I know how to handle it."

"Building it is one thing; sustaining it is another. You need to learn the difference."

I shake my head in disbelief. "I can't believe you're trying to control every aspect of my business."

"Isn't that the point of this arrangement? Your emotions will never let you see the bigger picture."

"The bigger picture looks like I'm only supposed to follow a script and nod like a puppet while you discuss the fate of my company?"

"Now you're just being stubborn. I'm offering experienced guidance. You're refusing it out of pride."

"No, it's not pride. It's called wanting to have a say in my own business."

"You'll lose more than your say if you keep this up. You'll lose the business itself."

Silence hangs heavily between us. I wonder if I'm on the wrong side of this argument. All I want is to protect King's with everything, so I can't just overlook the decision-making. But, at the same time, I'd come to Theo for help, and he must feel bad that I'm not trusting him completely with the affairs. Maybe I should take a step back.

No. I won't.

Theo has already stripped a huge chunk of my pride off me. I'll hold on to the last shred with everything I have.

"I won't lose my company. I won't let that happen," I say quietly, shaking my head.

"Then listen to those who can help you, even if it's hard to swallow."

"I can't just blindly follow your lead. I need to be part of the decisions."

"I'm not asking you to follow blindly. I'm asking you to trust that I have your best interests at heart."

"You have a peculiar way of showing it!" I snap, gesturing at my stained clothes and the cleaning supplies in the corner.

"Maybe I don't know how to show that I care, but at least I do." He protests.

"Trust is earned, Theo. And right now, it's hard to come by."

He tries again, this time more calmly. "Listen to me. I've been where you are and have even faced the same challenges. I know what it takes to navigate this world."

"But it's my world too. I can't keep letting you dictate how I run things."

"You don't have to do it alone. I'll say this the millionth time—I'm here to help, not hinder."

"Help or control? There's a fine line, and I feel like I'm dancing on it."

Theo's expression softens, a hint of frustration in his eyes. "I don't want to control you, but I won't watch you make mistakes that could cost you everything."

"I appreciate your concern, but I need to find my own way. I need the space to make decisions, even if they're not the ones you'd make."

Theo nods, "Whatever," he says. "I have a backup plan, but I'll need you to accompany me tomorrow."

I'm surprised, "Tomorrow?"

Chapter 6

He rolls his eyes, "Yes, tomorrow."
I blink, "But tomorrow is Sunday. I have plans with Kaylee."
He smirks, "Yes, I know. Is that a problem?"
I quickly shake my head. Saving King's might depend on this. "Not at all."
"Good, make sure you have the right outfit."
"Are you going to tell me where we're going?"
Theo turns, loosening his tie as he heads back to his study. "We'll be attending the Azure Gala."
My gasp is audible. Azure is not just a Gala. It's the only event in the world where power is a physical guest.

Chapter 7

Theodore

"Did you really invite Raya to accompany you for the evening?" Ethan questions, surprised.

"Of course, why not?" I reply.

It doesn't make sense to bring an actual date when these kind of events are all about networking. Plus, Raya is polite, friendly, and knowledgeable. She can hold her own in most conversations, making a great first impression. I'd choose that a hundred times over some pretty, over dressed dull head.

"I thought you'd find a proper date," he remarks, and I shoot him a glare. "What?"

"Ethan, this is a business gala. Business and pleasure are two lines that should never meet."

He shrugs, not constrained by the same rules. His past behavior of crossing the line with his Assistants has led to restrictions – no more sleeping with assistants, as mandated by the board.

"Raya will impress people."

He smirks, "Including old William?"

"Well, him too."

"Are you using poor Raya to win him over?"

Chapter 7

I ignore the comment; there's no need to dignify it with a response. Besides, he already knows the answer.

"You're going to owe her big time."

If she succeeds in getting him on board, I'll reward her with a promotion and a substantial bonus.

"You still haven't told her, have you?" Ethan probes.

"Told her what?"

"That you're just using her to revive King's before forcing her to sell it to you."

I brush him off, "Those are long term plans. If you actually think ahead like this when it comes to your business, maybe you'd have beaten me by now."

Ethan chuckles, "You're playing with fire, Theo. One day, that ruthlessness might come back to bite you."

I glance at my watch once again, ignoring Ethan. It's almost seven, and I start wondering where she is. Just as I'm about to give her a call, a black car pulls up in front. The driver steps out, nods at us, and goes to the back seat. When he opens the door, a long, tanned leg gracefully slides out, and a high-heeled foot touches the ground.

My attention is fully captured by this woman getting out of the car; I'm captivated. The driver offers his hand, and her delicate hand fits into his. I'm left speechless when I realize it's Raya stepping out. Her long, curly hair flows down her back. She's wearing a dark blue dress that hugs her figure perfectly, and there's a slit on her right side that goes from the bottom all the way up to her hip.

"Holy Mother of God." Ethan gapes, staring at Raya with his eyes almost popping out of their sockets.

"Get a hold of yourself and put your damn eyes back inside your sockets!" I give him a stern look.

"Theodore, I respect your self-control, truly. But, man, you've got to acknowledge a stunning woman when she walks in, and Raya is incredibly beautiful. She's the epitome of beauty. When did she change this much? Huh? This isn't the Raya I know from high school."

I inhale deeply. "Don't even entertain the idea of trying to approach her." I caution him. "You're not permitted to touch her. Heck, don't even try to flirt with my woman or I'll kill you."

"Your woman?" He raises an eyebrow.

"You know what I mean."

His lips tighten as his eyes narrow in my direction. I stand my ground, glaring back at him. "Fine, you're a jerk."

I casually shrug, "Nothing new there."

"The sooner you admit that you're interested in her, the easier it'll be for all of us. You do realize that every guy in this place is going to be trying to get her attention, right?"

"What?"

He chuckles, "She's incredibly attractive, Theodore. Every guy in here will want to pursue her. How are you going to handle it? Glare at them all night?"

If that's what I have to do to keep them away, then yes. "I don't know what you're talking about. She's free to make her own choices."

He starts to retort, likely with something foolish. "Except you," I interject quickly.

His eyes narrow into slits. "Jerk."

I flash a wide smile. "Exactly, now why don't you go enjoy your evening with your date? What's her name again? Zara?"

He raises his hands in surrender. "Fine." He steps back, shooting me a glare and a 'I'm watching you' signal.

I shift my focus to Raya, my mouth going dry as she grins at me. Descending the steps, I reach her at the bottom. "You look stunning," I murmur, kissing her cheek.

Blushing, she says, "Thank you, and thanks for the dress. You didn't have to buy it for me." She links her arm through mine, and we start walking up the stairs.

"I'm happy I did; it suits you."

She smiles, "Did I see Ethan with you?"

Chapter 7

I roll my eyes. "Yeah, he's in there somewhere with his date."

"Oh, is she terrible?"

I lean my head to the side, "Why would you think that?"

Her eyes widen slightly, and her lips part. "The way you mentioned he's with his date and rolled your eyes. I assumed you didn't like his date. Is that not the case?"

"I honestly haven't met her. After tonight, she and Ethan won't cross paths again so I stay away from his relationships. The last time I tried to be a great cousin, a deranged woman showed up at my work threatening me to call Ethan or she'll tear the place down."

"That's crazy. Do I have to avoid her too?" She sounds disappointed, and I stop to look at her, "If you're avoiding her, then I won't have anyone to talk to."

"You'll have me, and you can talk to them if you want."

"I'm here with you. I don't think I'll be comfortable with anyone else."

Something about the way Raya said that warms my chest. I smile, "Let me guess, you stopped going out as much since our breakup, right?"

"I don't."

"How then did you survive on your dates?"

"I didn't date."

"Really?"

"Really."

"Not a single date?" I press. "Burt from Chemistry?"

"Stop." Raya presses me with a glare that's hard enough to shut me up.

"I can hang with you all night," I offer. "You're the main character tonight."

She frowns, "Aren't you attending because you want to network? I thought the gala was for you to attract new investors for King's?"

I nod, "It is, but trust me, the people I'm targeting would rather talk to you than me. That's why you're here."

She seems puzzled, "What does that mean?"

"It means I can be difficult, and I've given them that impression in the past. We're here to meet William Heather, and he hasn't warmed up to me. On the other hand, you're polite, sweet, and can hold engaging conversations. You'll connect with him, and if he doesn't, then we don't need his investment."

She stares at me blankly for a moment, as if gathering her thoughts before speaking. "Theodore, I'm not experienced in seducing businessmen at parties. I don't think this is a good idea. What if I make a mistake?" She looks anxious now, her eyes wide and her hands shaky.

"Who says you're seducing him?"

"Isn't that the whole point of doing this at a party?"

I clench my fists. This woman always manages to get on my nerves. "Raya, listen to me. You are not here to seduce William Heather. If he makes the slightest move on you, you are to call me and I will punch his facial bones into dust."

"Okay," Raya nods nervously. "You're always ready to do that."

"I wanted to do it to Burt."

"Why?"

"If he didn't transfer so suddenly, he'd hate me."

"Why?"

I ignore her again. "I would have killed him," I say and quickly add before she asks why again. "And remember, this isn't everything. You're not here for a critical examination; you're here to enjoy yourself." I keep walking, and she holds onto my arm, her fingers pressing into my clothes and gripping my skin. She's anxious. "Take it easy. How about we grab a drink for you?"

She nods, "Yes, please."

I guide her through the entrance and into the bar. It's bustling already, with most people gathered here before the meal is served.

"There's William," I maneuver us past the throngs of people to William Heather's table.

William spots us coming and stands up to greet us. "Ah, Theodore, you've brought a delightful companion tonight," the old man says, noticing Raya for the first time. The way his eyes travel over her body and his

Chapter 7

pupils dilate makes me want to shove his head in the buffet, but I calm myself down.

"Thank you, Mr. Heather. It's an honor to be here," Raya says, blushing as I introduce them.

"Please, call me William. I may look old physically but I'm young at heart. And the pleasure is all mine. A woman as charming as you brings the joy and elegance to tiring gatherings like this. Come on, sit," William says, pulling out the seat closest to him for Raya and shunning his other guests off.

"That's very kind of you to say," Raya answers, sitting down. Uncomfortable, I pull out the chair on the other side and sit.

"Kindness has nothing to do with it. Beauty deserves recognition. Theodore, you're a lucky man."

I smile, "Indeed, I am."

William turns back to Raya, "So, tell me, what does a captivating woman like you do when she's not gracing events with her presence?"

"Well, I work with Theodore at King's Corporation. We're currently working on revitalizing the company."

"Admirable," William answers, nodding. "And what other interests fill your time?"

"Um, I enjoy reading, painting, and spending time with friends," she answers thoughtfully.

Is it just me, or have I gotten kicked out of their conversation?

William is grinning, "I must say, the image of you with a paintbrush in hand is quite enchanting. Perhaps you could paint a portrait for an old man like me?"

"I'm flattered, but I'm no professional artist." Raya giggles. Why the fuck is she blushing?

"Ah, but passion often surpasses skill. I'd be honored to sit for a portrait, no matter the outcome. Just give me a date and time."

Okay, this is getting too deep. "William, Raya is here to discuss business tonight. Perhaps we should focus on that."

William winks at Raya, "Of course, whatever this angel wants."

Annie Ireland

It turns out that you could convince William Heather to do anything—maybe even walk in the fire—if there's a beautiful woman involved.

As the night progresses, it becomes increasingly evident that the old man is more captivated by Raya than any business proposition. He seems enchanted, hanging on her every word until we have him wrapped around our finger.

Raya smiles at the end of the conversation. "Mr. Heather, it's been a pleasure talking with you. I appreciate your willingness to help."

"The pleasure is all mine, my dear," William grins and takes Raya's manicured hand, planting a kiss on it. My eyes twitch. "I must say, I haven't enjoyed a conversation this much in years.

I've had enough of this bullshit.

"That's enough, Raya," I cut in, snatching Raya's hand and ignoring her surprised look. "We need to circulate and talk to others."

Raya is taken aback but she turns to Mr. Heather again, "Mr. Heather, it was truly delightful talking to you. I'll hold you up on that painting appointment."

"The pleasure was mine. I'll be looking forward to our session."

As we step away from William's table, I grab Raya's arm and pull her towards the exit. Raya winces at the tightness of my grip.

"Theo, what's gotten into you?" She protests, snatching her hand.

"Don't play coy. I know exactly what you were doing back there."

"What are you talking about?"

"Flirting with William Heather! That's what you were doing. This isn't some game, Raya. We're here for King's, not for you to entertain wealthy old men and offer to paint them," I accuse her, loosening my collar as the weather has grown incredibly hot all of a sudden. "You have never even offered to paint me!"

"Theo, I was just being polite. There's no need to act like this," Raya sounds upset but she's calm. "Wasn't it your idea in the first place?"

Raya is right. This was all my idea so I don't get why I'm reacting this way. I thought I'd be able to handle it but something about this round-

Chapter 7

faced, stubborn woman always has me doing this I normally wouldn't do. Is this part of the power Ethan was talking about?

"Or didn't you say I had to charm him into investing with us?"

I sneer. "It looked more like you were enjoying his attention a bit too much."

Raya throws her hands up in frustration. "I can't believe you're accusing me of intentionally flirting. I'm not a child, Theo. I know why we're here."

"Well, act like it then."

By the time we reach the exit, the tension is thick. I call for my driver in frustration, and when the limo arrives, I gesture for Raya to get in.

"I'm not getting in until I get an apology, Theodore Harry Caddel!" Raya declares, folding her arms in defiance. Her face is puffed, cute, like a baby's.

"I should be getting the apology," I retort.

"No. You've insulted me far too much, and you don't have the right to dictate who I talk to or how I behave."

"No right?" I scoff.

"Yes. I'm not yours to control. I can choose to be with whoever I want."

"Your clever retorts won't change the fact that I've claimed you as mine."

"I'm not an object!"

"True, but you didn't seem to mind submission when I was pounding into you and your fingers were digging into my skin," In one swift movement, I cover the space between us, and her back is pressing against the waiting car. "Shall I give you a reminder?"

Raya's face turns a deep shade of red, and she struggles to find the right words. "You... You can't just bring that up to win an argument. It's not fair."

My resentment boils over as I retort, "What's not fair is enduring a relentless hard-on while I watch you enjoy yourself with other men. While you're all smiles and laughter, I'm stuck with vivid fantasies of you riding me and losing control and you coming all over my face and my cock."

Raya's opens her mouth but no words come out. She's red as a tomato. I want to see her ass cheeks go red when I spank her for being such a trouble maker. My gaz is intense as I command, "Get in the damn car, Raya. We're not done tonight, and I intend to make sure of that."

Chapter 8

Raya

Once safely inside the limo with the door shut, Theodore directs his driver to head to his apartment. The privacy panel goes up, and he pulls me onto his lap, his lips seeking mine, exploring every inch with his probing tongue. My moans escape as my hands clutch at the lapels of his jacket.

I desperately need to tear them off him, but fear of the cost stops me.

"God, you're stunning, baby," Theodore murmurs, peppering kisses along my neck. His hand moves between my breasts, kneading and caressing, while the other glides along my outer thigh.

As pleasure intensifies, I find myself gasping and breathing heavily, my curvy body trembling as Theodore spreads my legs on either side of his waist.

I avert my gaze, long lashes lowered, a blush warming my skin with the knowledge that I'm not wearing anything underneath my dress.

"Fuck, you are so beautiful."

He lifts me effortlessly, cradling me against his chest, making me feel weightless—though I'm a bit on the chubby side and have a soft spot for cookies and ice cream. Yet, he straddles me without any strain.

Then, he resumed kissing me, his mouth avidly exploring mine, eliciting a needy moan from my lips. I sense his firm body pressed against mine, a sizable bulge pressing into my hip. His hands roam up and down my curves possessively, stealing my breath away.

Then Theodore breaks the kiss.

"Can you feel how much I crave you? How hard I am? It's been building up all day, Raya," he pants, his words a heated whisper against my ear.

I gasp, my cheeks deepening with a blush. "Part your legs for me, baby. Let's see if this excites you as much as it does me."

I glance down at him and follow his request, hesitantly opening my legs, causing my dress to ride up a little bit more

Theodore keeps me close, and I feel one of his hands leave my hips, descending lower and lower until it rests between my thighs.

I clamp them together, blocking its path, but he gently coaxes them open again.

"It's okay. I'll be gentle for now," he growls.

I hide my face in his shoulder as his fingers trail up my inner thighs, brushing against the damp fabric of my panties.

"Damn, baby," he groans, lips meeting my neck and his finger finding the wet spot. I shudder at the gentle touch, anxiety, and excitement flooding me as he discovers the effect he has on me.

"I can't believe I've made you this wet with just a kiss," he remarks, pulling back slightly. I gather my courage, meeting his gaze and sealing his words with another deep kiss.

He maneuvers me on top of him, rucking up my dress around my waist. His hands knead my backside, guiding me down onto the firm bulge of his cock. I feel it twitch against me, and a surprised moan escapes me. I didn't anticipate it would feel like this.

Theodore guides me, rubbing my sensitive area against his arousal, and I can't help but moan. My body responds intensely—my sensitive spot pulsating and my muscles contracting.

"Move against me, baby. Let yourself feel this pleasure," he grunts, locking his lips with mine in a demanding kiss. His tongue explores my mouth, seeking entrance.

Chapter 8

I yield to him, letting my body press closely against his larger frame. He persists in stimulating me with his firm erection until I reach a powerful climax, the sensation almost overwhelming.

I sense Theodore's arms enveloping me, pulling me closer to him. I nestle against him, my hands reaching around his back, drawing him in even tighter.

He offers a slight smile and shifts from dry humping to gently caressing my breasts, simultaneously engaging in a deep, fervent kiss. A moan escapes my lips as my hands tightly grip his robust, muscular chest, fingers pressing into his skin.

I feel his finger tracing circles on my clit, and then it goes lower, slipping beyond my entrance, causing me to recoil from his touch.

A strong, wet pleasure fills me, stirring newfound desires and a longing for a connection with the man I want to hate but can't.

"You're so wet and goddamn tight, baby. If you're this good with my fingers, I can't wait to feel you around my cock. It's enough to make me want to come just thinking about it."

He moves against me, his firm erection pressed between us, nudging my belly.

"Baby, you climaxed too quickly," he comments, rolling us over until I'm on my back with him hovering above me.

I take a deep breath. "What?" I ask, smiling.

This man has a way of touching me that feels almost magical. I'm not sure how many times he's made me climax since our first sex in High school, but I'm definitely not complaining, and I won't object to whatever he wants to do right now.

"Well, it's pretty simple: I'll just have to do it all over again," he breathes against my sensitive spot, his tongue immediately starting to circle and tease it.

I hold his head close to my clit with both hands, a moan escaping my lips. "Oh, Theo... please!"

He licks me slowly, mischief glistening in his eyes. It's like I'm the most delightful thing he's ever tasted. The dark, bristly stubble on his jaw tickles the inside of my thigh.

"Tell me what you want, baby," he says as his gentle movements keep me on the edge.

I guide him downward. "Don't tease me, please."

He smirks at me. "I won't, and I'll make you come so hard you'll feel it for days."

I close my eyes, whimpering at his words, a promise and a threat simultaneously. I try to think of a witty reply, but any comeback I had in mind fades away as Theodore's tongue thrusts into me in one swift motion, rapidly moving in and out.

My moans echo in the car, and Theodore's satisfied grunts only intensify my arousal. Soon, he shifts, and now two of his fingers are penetrating me while his skilled tongue gives my clit playful side-to-side licks.

Before I realize what's happening, my body is reaching another climax, and Theodore is ascending my body, his erection in hand, his fingers briskly stroking the substantial length.

He kneels beside me, gazing down with intense desire in his eyes.

"I would have made you choke on my cock, but I can't wait anymore," he groans. "I want to have you here in this car. I don't care if the driver hears us."

Before I knew it, Theodore had switched positions with me, making me climb him. Now, I'm entirely bare, straddling his hot, eager body and descending onto his enormous, bulging shaft. My pussy bursts into a myriad of hot feelings, pleasure pulsating at my clit and tingling in my nipples upon impact.

Theodore helps himself up, balancing on one arm, and I envelop myself entirely around him, arms and legs clinging to him desperately. His own arms snake around me as he starts thrusting upward every time I ride him downward, reaching so deeply that we both pant in ecstasy.

The world fades away, forgotten, slipping from our reality, and now there's only us. Nothing else is real or matters anymore.

We ascend together as our climax slowly builds, hands exploring, lips

Chapter 8

tasting, the moist sounds of our bodies slapping together filling the car alongside my moans and his groans of pleasure.

A few more thrusts and we both succumb, our orgasms engulfing us. Theodore eases back down the bed, with me still atop him, wrapped around his body.

"That was incredible, love," he says, breathing heavily.

"Yeah," I say, breathing heavily.

"But we're not done yet. I still have more planned for you."

Theodore fulfills his promise as soon as we get home.

I have barely stepped inside the door when he seizes me, crushing his mouth against mine. The kiss is a hot blend of anger and demand, overwhelming in its intensity.

I kiss him back just as intensely, telling him I want all the passion he's got. We end up in the kitchen, and our kiss pushes me against the fridge. I lean into him, feeling the cold fridge against my back.

"What are you doing to me?" Theodore growls, his voice a deep rumble.

"I don't know, but you're doing the same thing to me," I reply breathlessly.

Our lips meet once more, and I sway my hips in tandem with Theodore. The passion between us is undeniable, and it's worrisome how effortlessly Theodore ignites the raging animal in me. When our kiss breaks, he rips my dress, and I gasp.

"That cost a fortune!"

"I'll buy you a hundred more," he promises, pleased with himself as he guides me to the bedroom.

Moments later, I shed his clothes, and we slide beneath the comforting embrace of the sheets.

In the bedroom, we passionately roll around the bed, biting and pulling at each other in a thrilling dance of pleasure. My breasts brush against Theodore's eager mouth as we move together energetically, the pace unrestrained, only stopping when we both reach the peak of our intense climax.

Annie Ireland

* * *

The first wave of regret washes over me first thing in the morning. My eyes fly open and take the room in.

Of course, it wasn't a dream, you fool.

Theodore is still peacefully sleeping beside me, so I can groan and knock my head in peace without worrying that I'd look like a crazy lady.

I stop when my head starts to ache, deciding that's enough punishment for now. Theodore is unmoving, deep in the kind of sleep nobody wants to wake up from. There's a small smile playing on his lips. I observe his sleeping form, realizing that nothing has changed. I can't envision anything serious with him.

When he stirs, I swiftly get out of bed, heading to my room to change before deciding to get busy to stop the torrents of thoughts from overwhelming me.

Downstairs, I encounter the housekeeper, who greets me with a knowing look. "Good morning, Miss. I'm Mrs. Johnson, the housekeeper," she says with a warm smile.

Finally. Someone I can get along with in this house.

Mrs. Johnson seems nice. With silver hair neatly tied back, she gives off a motherly vibe. I immediately wanted to be friends with her.

"Morning, Mrs. Johnson. Nice to meet you. Call me Raya," I reply with a broader smile.

"I came up earlier to ask what you'd like to have for breakfast, but you weren't in your room," she says.

"Oh, I … um," I stammer, suddenly at a loss for words as a blush creeps up my neck.

"It's okay, sweetheart," she says, winking.

Fuck. Now the housekeeper knows I fucked Theodore.

"Any chance I could give cooking a shot today?"

Mrs. Johnson chuckles, "Well, I suppose if Mr. Caddel doesn't mind, we could let you have a go at it."

I nod appreciatively, "Great! What's on the menu?"

Chapter 8

"We were thinking of a simple breakfast – scrambled eggs, toast, and maybe some fresh fruit," she suggests.

"Perfect. Let's do it," I say, feeling more at ease.

As we work together in the kitchen, Mrs. Johnson guides me through the process of making scrambled eggs. I crack the eggs into a bowl, and she shows me how to whisk them until they blend nicely. The sizzle of butter in the pan is oddly comforting.

"Mr. Theodore usually prefers his eggs with a dash of hot sauce," Mrs. Johnson mentions.

I grin, "Got it. Spicy eggs it is."

While the eggs cook, she toasts some bread and slices fresh fruit. As we set the table, I ask, "You seem so comfortable with me. Do you do this often?"

"Do what?"

"This whole ... bonding thingy with Theodore's women."

Mrs. Johnson chuckles softly. "Darling, Mr. Caddel hardly ever brings anyone home. This is a rare sight."

Surprised, I ask, "Really? I thought..."

"Oh, no. It's not a regular occurrence," she interrupts, her hands skillfully managing the cooking. "I was quite shocked, to be honest. When I heard someone in the house, I almost thought we had a burglar. Imagine my surprise when I saw your face and recognized you from the picture."

Curious, I ask, "Picture? What picture?"

Before Mrs. Johnson can respond, Theodore's gruff morning voice cuts in. "What's going on here?" he asks, entering the room with a slightly disheveled appearance. His hair is flying all over the place, his shirt inside out, and his joggers hanging dangerously low.

There's a light, rosy hue to his cheeks from the chilly air of the Air conditioner in his room. God, he's so handsome it makes me want to sigh like a teenage girl.

He gives the kitchen a quick once-over and then spots us. With a crooked smile on his face, he makes eye contact with me and approaches.

"Thought you were trying to burn my house down again. Morning, Mrs. Johnson," he calls.

"Mr. Caddel, I hope you had a wonderful night," Mrs. Johnson grins, momentarily taking her attention off cooking.

"I did." Theo's voice is low, and his dark gaze is on me. I know what he's thinking. He's undoubtedly thinking about our time together last night, brainstorming ways to make it even more memorable. His composed adult mindset seems to have vanished, replaced by a more spontaneous and unpredictable demeanor.

He'll not do anything crazy here, will he?

"You know what, though?" Theo finally asks after observing me in silence for a while. "Let's do something different."

"Are you in the mood to eat something else, Mr. Caddel?"

"Yes, but I'd like to make it myself, so if you'd excuse us, Mrs. Johnson."

Mrs. Johnson hesitates, looking between me and Theo like she's sensing something unusual between us. Eventually, she decides to leave. Theo turns to me, a mischievous glint in his eyes.

"I'm thinking ... um ..." Theo is saying, tapping his chin like he's deep in thought. "Aha! A gourmet meal. What do you think?"

"What happens to Mrs. Johnson's effort?" I ask crossly. He's so unbelievable.

Theo feigns innocence. "What about it?"

I narrow my eyes. "So you'll just waste all of these?"

He grins, unrepentant. "It's not wasting; it's just simply elevating breakfast. Besides, Mrs. Johnson will understand."

I huff, disappointed. "You're unbelievable."

He chuckles. "That's why you love me."

I roll my eyes. "Debatable."

Shaking my head, I start to gather the scrambled eggs and fresh fruits. Theo watches me in confusion. It isn't until I dish it into a disposable plastic and begin to take it out of the kitchen that he realizes my intention to eat alone upstairs.

Chapter 8

"Raya?" He calls. "Come on, loosen up a bit," he teases, attempting to drape an apron around me.

I swat his hands away. "If you have nobody to teach you basic manners and how not to be so arrogant, I'll gladly do it."

"Jesus. You're being so hard on me over breakfast?! It's just food!"

I clench my fists, frustrated. "The point always manages to fly over your head, doesn't it? It's not about the food; it's about respecting others."

He sighs, realizing the depth of my displeasure. "Okay, maybe I went too far. I'm sorry."

I glare at him, but I don't say anything. Then he raises his hands in surrender. "Look, you're stubborn, but I don't want to eat alone. Let's compromise. We'll enjoy this meal together, and next time, we'll consider my gourmet offer. I'm sorry."

"Fine."

He sweeps his hand across his face, shaking his head. "Do you understand you've nearly caused me a heart attack these recent days?"

"If you weren't so stubborn, perhaps I wouldn't have had to push you to the brink of insanity."

"I don't buy that at all. I'm convinced you would have still driven me mad. You must hate me so fucking much."

"Fair point," I shrug. "I probably would have."

"Oddly enough, it's one of the things that attracts me to you. You give me shit."

"Only when you deserve it," I retort. He laughs, but I'm not done with my tantrum. Happy that I had my way this time, I flip my hair in his face dramatically and sashay back into the kitchen, feeling his eyes pressing into my back.

Ha, take that, you fucking jerk.

NINE.

Theo

Of all the people to have feelings for, it had to be the most stubborn woman in New York City.

Sitting behind the desk in my office, I stare blankly at my screen and consider all the sorry motherfuckers who must be in the same situation as me. They'd be formerly dignified men with well-established egos, slowly losing their heads because of one woman they can't seem to let go.

I catch a glimpse of myself in the mirrored wall on my left. I've really lost all my bad, ruthless man charm. Now I'm just—Jesus, I'm gone. I'm a fucking simp now.

Hell.

I press my hand to my forehead, a small smile stretching my lips. This shouldn't be funny, but it is. Who would have thought I'd ever let anyone other than myself determine how I feel, emotionally and physically?

I've engaged in self-pleasure twice daily throughout the entire week. However, whenever I'm in Raya's presence, which is quite frequent, it feels like there's a blockage, and the mounting pressure leads to frustration.

Strangely, nightclubs don't appeal to me; instead, I opt to stay home with a drink in hand, watching a random TV show and texting Raya since she refused to join come downstairs to hang out.

I'm not someone who typically engages in texting. Never have been. But, man, when I notice her name appearing on my phone, it's like... damn, I can't help but feel giddy. And whenever she takes a long time to reply, like she's doing now, I get all worked up.

What's up with that?

I shouldn't feel so thrilled about getting a text, especially considering our conversations lack any importance. While there are occasional messages about King's company, the majority involve her sharing something positive, and I respond by being a dick about it, leading to her getting upset.

The tension between us is escalating at an alarming pace, and I'm aware that I should likely step back from this precarious precipice. I should reclaim control of whatever influence she has over me.

I should stay away, but for some reason, I find myself unable to resist.

The rational part of me insists I stop dwelling on her, but it's proving

Chapter 8

to be an impossible feat. I'm fully aware that I'm frustrating her, yet stopping myself remains an elusive task.

Hell... when did all my thoughts become all about one girl?

Perhaps the moment she walked into my office that day was the warning sign I overlooked. I should have realized then that she was destined to unravel me.

Lost in contemplation, I reach behind my desk, fingers brushing against all the folders there until I find the one marked "Kings." Damn, was it always this heavy, or is it some psychological effect on my fear of even touching the document?

Fuck, I need to pull my head out of my ass when it comes to business, but it's no easy feat, so I dial Eric and inform him that I have the documents related to acquiring Raya's company and pause. He hesitates before responding.

"Okayyy," Eric drags his 'okay' unexcitedly like he's expecting me to go on, but when I don't, he asks. "Are you ready to sign?"

I sigh. "My head's still deep in my ass."

"Okay, what the fuck?"

"You know what I mean," I grit my teeth.

He chuckles, sensing my dilemma. "You've got to make a decision, my friend. What does your gut tell you?"

How do I tell him that right now, my gut is telling me to fling these papers out the window without sounding like a simp? I lean back in my chair, conflicted. "It's not just about the deal. It's more complicated." It seems like a better approach, but Eric doesn't seem to understand it yet.

He becomes serious, "Complications are part of the game. I shouldn't need to tell you that. But at the end of the day, what matters most to you?"

I consider his question carefully. "I don't know if it's about the money or something else if that's what you're asking."

"Ah, so it's the heart versus the wallet battle," Eric replies knowingly. Then, after a while, he says, "Listen, my advice is this: Follow your heart. You don't want to regret this decision down the line. Money is essential, but it's not the only currency life deals in."

"What if my heart and my wallet aren't aligned?"

"Then you need to question what truly matters to you. Is it the immediate gains or the long-term fulfillment?"

"What if choosing my heart leads to complications at the end of the day?"

Since when did I become this clueless?

Eric's voice grows firm, "Life is uncertain. It's how you find your way through that uncertainty that defines you. Don't be afraid to choose something beyond those dollars and cents. Sometimes, the most rewarding decisions come with risks. Listen, I gotta go now. Vicky's here, and you know what that means. Bye."

The call just ends with a click, and I don't even get to say anything. I feel like cussing at Eric because now I'm more confused than before. But I get it; if Vicky's there, it means one of two things. Either he's gotten himself into some kind of trouble for throwing shades at her husband since he never liked the man, or he's about to get loads of work dumped on his ass. Just because I'm a hater, I pray it's the former.

I start to glance through the papers when there's a gentle knock on my door. Raya walks into my office, and I swiftly put the documents away. She raises her eyebrow at the suspicious sight.

"Took you long enough."

Raya rolls her eyes. "I've been stuck in nanny duties all day," she says with so much hate that something shivers within me. "I assumed whatever you had to say wasn't important, or you would have bothered to come downstairs."

"I could have been dying."

"Next time you're on your deathbed, and I happen to care enough to open your text, share your last wishes so I won't feel guilty about not reaching out."

"Harsh but fair."

"What do you want, Theo?"

"Lunch together."

She pauses and then says, "No."

Chapter 8

"Fresh air won't kill you."

"Do you know the type of fresh air I appreciate?" she retorts. "The kind that doesn't make me breathe in damp rags and dust from your ridiculous paintings and cabinets!"

"Raya," I say tiredly—pleadingly. "Just get dressed, will you? Please?"

An irritated groan falls from her lips before she spins on her heels and leaves. That woman sure does know how to keep me on my toes because that's how I spend the next one hour, praying she comes out of her room dressed up.

Unable to endure the suspense any longer, I knock on her bedroom door and swing it open just as Raya attempts to do the same from the inside. There's a momentary pause as I take her in—she's adorned in the sexiest sundress I've ever seen, paired with high-ankle boots, and... oh, no.

"Why is it so low?" I ask, pointing at her chest.

She glances down and then back at me. "Um, that's how sundresses come?"

My brow soars. "Are you trying to give me a coronary? I can see your entire cleavage." I bend a little.

"Need I remind you that we're not a thing, Theo? The fact that we've been screwing doesn't give you the right to complain about my dresses like you own the body underneath. Should we go now, or shall I turn back?"

She steps around me and strides ahead of me toward my waiting Lamborghini, leaving me with no choice but to follow suit. The engine purrs to life as we drive to the restaurant in silence.

It's a little crowded in there, but I'm glad my usual table is empty. A brown-haired woman dressed in their uniform comes to welcome us.

"Your seat's that way, Mr. Caddel," she says.

"Thank you." I glance back at Raya, who's walking behind me before we head toward the back of the restaurant. She weaves us through the sitting area and sits us next to a window, offering a street view.

"You're a piece of work," I say to Raya once the woman takes our orders and leaves. I can't hold it back anymore.

Raya gives me a stern look. "No, you are the piece of work. And it's why I broke up with you in the first place."

I frown, feeling defensive. "Don't judge me so harshly."

She crosses her arms. "Why wouldn't I when you haven't even tried to change?"

"I've cut down on partying, started to read more books, established a charity foundation, and I'm more patient now."

She raises an eyebrow. "Is that it?"

I pause, eyeing her. "I've been working on communicating better and controlling my temper."

Raya waits, "And?"

I rack my brain. I know this woman is doing significant damage to my tough exterior, but I didn't expect her to have me trying—and wanting—to list all the good things I've done. "I've been more supportive and understanding."

She sighs. "Anything else?"

I hesitate before admitting, "I've been trying to be more considerate and less self-centered."

Raya nods slowly, but I can tell she isn't satisfied. "You're not smoking still, are

you? Have you finally realized it's bad for you?"

The waiter arrives at our table, balancing a tray with our lunch dishes. He wears a friendly smile as he places the plates before us, skillfully describing each dish with enthusiasm. The aroma of the freshly served food fills the air and makes my stomach rumble in anticipation. Dealing with Raya had made me forget how hungry I was. We exchange polite nods of appreciation as he leaves, and we can finally continue our conversation.

"Do you realize what's really going to harm me? You."

"Me?" she inquires, and oh, how I wish I could capture the expression on her face. I adore the way she reacts when I surprise her.

"Yes, you."

"How will I harm you?"

Chapter 8

I massage my scalp with my fingers, offering a bit of relief. "You're attempting to eradicate all my bad habits. It's not healthy for me, and it's tarnishing my image."

"Oh," she says in a gentle tone. "You don't have to rely on smoking and drinking to maintain your image, you know."

"And how else should people see me as a rebel without a whiskey in one hand and a cigarette in the other?"

"You don't require props to portray a bad boy image, Theo; it's all about the attitude."

"Attitude is nothing next to appearance. I like my props, as you mentioned."

"Those props will cut your life in half."

"Well, I might as well enjoy the life I have now," I respond. "And what about you?"

"Me?"

"You think you're all perfect, don't you?" I query. "How about you learn how to cook and stop trying to commit murder whenever you enter the kitchen?"

Raya scoffs. "I'm not that bad."

I arch an eyebrow. "Remember that lasagna incident in High school? And your extra crispy pancakes? I thought I was eating volcanic ash."

She rolls her eyes. "Okay, maybe I need a few more cooking lessons, but it doesn't make me any less of a person."

"A few? More like a culinary boot camp," I chuckle.

She pouts. "Fine. If it's that bad, maybe you should just hire a professional chef or have Mrs. Johnson cook all your meals."

"A professional chef?" I dramatically gasp, placing my hands on my chest. "Are you suggesting that my life is at risk every time you handle a spatula?"

Raya laughs. "You exaggerate, Theo."

"I beg to differ. I just fear for my taste buds. They deserve better."

"You just love to complain."

"But seriously," I continue, "what if we get a professional chef? We could have gourmet meals every day, and I won't have to fear for my life every time I sit down to eat."

Raya raises an eyebrow. "You're that worried about my cooking?"

"Yes. Yes, I am."

"Then do as you wish," she says and shrugs indifferently, even though I know she's getting upset. "Can I tell you a story, though?"

"The food's getting cold, but fire on."

"My friend Kaylee had a boyfriend about a year ago, and she was convinced he was the perfect match. They were the most adorable pair I'd ever witnessed. He was handsome, exuded this strong alpha male vibe—impressive chest, muscular arms, incredibly handsome—"

"Enough, I got it."

She chuckles and clears her throat. "Really attractive. But there was one big issue," she pauses, and her eyes twinkle, making me raise my eyebrows. "He was a walking chimney. Could fry his entire organs in one day if he had the chance."

I raise an eyebrow.

"Anyway, they waited for about a month and a half before doing the deed, but the atmosphere between them was incredibly intense. There was a constant exchange of banter, touches, and kisses, yet they never fully crossed that line. Whenever I was in the room with them, it felt like the air was on the verge of collapsing due to the tension. The way they looked at each other... I don't know why they delayed it, but it felt like torture for everyone nearby."

Hmmm.

"And then, after an intense game night, they went back to Kaylee's apartment and finally did it. Or so we assumed. Kaylee called the next day, informing me that she had finally been intimate with Jameson and ended their relationship that morning. When I inquired about the reason, she explained that the sexual experience was everything she could have desired: huge cock, attentive to her body, leaving marks in all the right places. The chemistry was present, the rhythm was set, the sounds of

Chapter 8

passion, the expressions of pleasure, but when it came down to it, neither of them could reach climax. It felt as though they were on the edge for hours, struggling to find release. Eventually, they each took matters into their own hands before going to sleep. By morning, they realized they weren't sexually compatible, leading to their decision to end the relationship."

What the hell is she going on about?

"So, let me get this straight. They were into each other; everything seemed perfect, yet they couldn't reach sexual satisfaction?"

"Exactly. Isn't that unfortunate? What if that's you in, say, the end of the year?"

"It can't be. I already know how to get you to orgasm. Remember?"

"Yeah, and Jameson thought the same. He boasted about his sexual prowess until his smoking became excessive. I don't even think size matters much. Kaylee mentioned Jameson had a large penis, so compared to you, you might be even worse."

"Hold on." I sit up straight. "Are you suggesting that you don't believe I have a large penis?"

She shrugs. "Big is subjective if you ask me."

I blink, feeling utterly confused. I don't understand what's happening, but I'm not enjoying it. She's speculating that smoking might impact my sexual performance, and now she's insinuating that I don't have a sufficiently large penis for her satisfaction. Who is this person, and what has she done to Raya Kings?

"I... " Damn, I don't even know how to react, and before I can find words, she starts to laugh. If I weren't so unsettled, I might join in, but instead, I patiently wait for her laughter to subside.

"Oh, Theo... that's how to embellish a story. Now you know how it feels when you exaggerate my bad cooking. You should see your face."

Damn it. I bite my bottom lip, attempting not to smile.

"Alright, the food's gone cold," Raya says.."We should eat."

And she starts to dig in before I can form any coherent words.

She outplayed me. Damn, did she outplay me, and strangely, I enjoyed every damn moment of it. Well, except for when I thought she questioned my penis.

TEN
Raya

"You're finally awake," Theo's voice slithers into my ears and breaks the residue of sleep away from my eyes.

He sounds so close.

I turn in bed, sheets twisting around my legs. Sunlight seeps through a gap in the curtains, and the scent of Theo's shampoo wafts through the room as I attempt to orient myself. My eyes slowly open, burdened by fatigue, adapting to the morning light. It's then that I recognize my surroundings. I sit up abruptly, glancing at my left.

Theo is there, naked from his waist up. With weary eyes, he gazes up at me from the bed. He appears stiff, not just physically, but his face is set in metal, too – everything except his eyes, which indicate worry. They dissolve once they see I'm awake. "I've been waiting for you," he says, then slips under the covers. "About yesterday, when you talked about my dick size ... you were joking, right?"

I groan, sitting up. This man is unbelievable. He'd clearly stayed up all night thinking about this. I bite back the urge to laugh, so I ask indifferently with an eye roll, "Would it make you feel better if I was joking?"

"I'd prefer for you not to hurt my ego this way," he pleads.

I lean back, feigning nonchalance. "Well, a girl's got to keep you on your toes, doesn't she?"

He scowls, clearly displeased. "This isn't time to joke, Raya."

I tilt my head, a sly smile playing on my lips. "Maybe I was joking. Maybe I wasn't."

His frustration grows, and he retorts darkly, "You don't know what you're playing with, Raya. I might just have to show you myself."

Despite his serious tone, I feel a sudden thrill, a shiver of anticipation running down my spine.

I've experienced desire around this man countless times, but this instance feels different – an overwhelming intensity as if I might burst out

Chapter 8

of my skin with need. I can't decipher if it's the gravity of his serious intent or the anticipation of him trying even harder to impress me. That's already an impossible feat, but it won't hurt to try.

He narrows the gap between us, kissing me passionately. I go for the fastening of his trousers, undoing the two buttons to reveal the hidden zipper. He tightens.

"I need this," I murmur against his lips. "Let me have this."

He doesn't ease up, but he doesn't resist either. As he sinks into my hands, a groan escapes him – a mix of pain and arousal. Gently, I squeeze him, intentionally tender, as I gauge him with my hands. He's hard, like stone, and warm. Running both my palms along his length, from base to tip, I catch my breath as he shudders beneath me.

Theo clasps my thighs, his hands gliding upward beneath the hem of my nightdress until his thumbs locate the black lace of my thong.

"Hmm," he mumbles against my lips. "I want to open you up and lick you until you plead for my cock."

"I could beg right now if you'd like." I caress him with one hand while using the other to reach toward his dresser, swiftly grabbing a condom.

One of his thumbs slips beneath the edge of my panties, the pad smoothly moving through the wetness of my core. "I've scarcely done anything for you," he whispers, his eyes glinting up at me in the shadows of the dim room, "and you're already so wet and eager for me."

"I can't stop myself."

"I don't want you to stop yourself." He slides two of his fingers inside me at once, letting out a groan when my walls clench around him helplessly. "It'll be unfair when it's my turn, and I can't stop."

I tear the foil packet open with my teeth and extend it to him, the ring of the condom protruding from the tear. "I'm not good with these."

His hand wraps around mine. "I'm breaking all my rules with you."

The gravity of his low tone sends a surge of warmth and confidence through me.

"Rules are meant to be shattered."

I catch the gleam of his teeth, and my cheeks warm. I'm eager to have him. Placing my hands on his shoulders for balance, I rise onto my knees, lifting to achieve the height needed to hover over the crown of Theo's sturdy erection. His hands clench at my hips, and I hear a snap as he forcefully removes my panties. The sudden sound and the assertive action intensified my desire to a fever pitch.

"Take it slow," he directs hoarsely, lifting his hips to push his pants down further.

His arousal glides between my legs as he moves, and I whimper, feeling achingly empty as if the orgasms he's given me earlier have only intensified my desire rather than satisfied it.

He tenses when I encircle him with my fingers and position him, nestling the broad crest against the moist folds of my cleft. The scent of our desire hangs heavy and humid in the air, a tempting blend of need and pheromones that stirs every cell in my body. My skin is flushed and tingling, my breasts feeling weighty and sensitive.

This is what I've been craving since the last time we were together—to claim him, to ascend his magnificent form, and take him deep inside me repeatedly.

"God. Raya," he gasps as I lower onto him, his hands flexing restlessly on my thighs.

I shut my eyes, feeling overly exposed. I desire intimacy with him, but this feels too personal. We are eye-to-eye, only inches apart, enclosed in our own space, with the rest of the world frozen around us. This is more than sex. It's love-making. And it's something more either of us are ready to handle. I can sense his unease, understanding he feels as off-center as I do.

"You're so beautiful." His gasped words carry a hint of delightful agony.

I take more of him, allowing him to slide deeper. I inhale deeply, feeling exquisitely stretched. "You're gigantic."

Placing his palm flat against my lower belly, he makes contact with my pulsating clit using the pad of his thumb, gently massaging it in unhurried, skillfully soft circles. Every part of my core constricts and contracts, drawing him in deeper.

Chapter 8

Opening my eyes, I peer at him from under heavy eyelids. He rests beneath me, his sturdy body tense with the instinctual desire to mate.

His neck curves, his head pushing into the bed as if he's resisting unseen restraints. "Ah, Damn," he utters, his teeth grinding. "I'm going to fill you up so bad."

The potent commitment excites me. Perspiration blankets my skin. I become moist and overheated, gliding seamlessly down the extent of his cock until I've almost completely enveloped him. A breathless cry slips out before I've fully taken him in. He's so deep inside me that it's almost unbearable, leading me to sway from side to side in an attempt to ease the unforeseen discomfort. Yet, my body appears unfazed by his size. It wraps around him, contracting, shivering on the brink of climax.

Theodore swears and clutches my hip with his unrestrained hand, encouraging me to lean backward as his chest rises and falls with hurried breaths. This adjustment changed my descent, and I willingly took in all of him. Instantly, his body temperature elevates, his upper body emitting a warm, sultry heat through his clothing. Drops of sweat appear on his upper lip.

Inclining forward, I run my tongue along the well-defined curve, savoring the saltiness with a soft murmur of pleasure. His hips churn eagerly. I lift cautiously, moving up a few inches before he halts me with that intense grip on my hip.

"Take it slow," he cautions once more, an authoritative edge that ignites a surge of lust within me.

I lower myself again, bringing him into me once more, experiencing a strangely delightful soreness as he pushes just beyond my boundaries. Our gaze remains locked as pleasure emanates from our connection. It occurs to me that we are both fully dressed, except for the most private and intimate areas of our bodies. I find this intensely sensual, much like the sounds he produces as if the pleasure is as intense for him as it is for me.

Passionately desiring him, I plant my lips on his, my fingers tightly clutching the sweat-moistened roots of his hair. I engage in a fervent kiss while swaying my hips, surrendering to the tantalizing rotation of his thumb, sensing the climax intensifying with each thrust of his lengthy, substantial member into my yielding center. I succumb to primal instincts, losing myself in the process.

I can't concentrate on anything but the intense desire to make love, the powerful need to ride his cock until the tension breaks and liberates me from this relentless hunger.

"It's so good," I sob, surrendering to him completely. "You feel... Ah, Christ, it feels too good."

Using both hands, Theo directs my rhythm, angling me in a way that has the large head of his cock caressing a tender, throbbing spot inside me. As I tighten and shake, I realize I'm going to climax from that, just from his hard thrusts inside me. "Theodore."

Grasping me firmly by the nape, he traps me as the orgasm surges through, initiating the euphoric spasms at my core and extending outward until I tremble all over. He observes me unravel, maintaining eye contact at a moment when I might have closed my eyes.

Engulfed in the intensity of his gaze, I emit a moan and experience a climax more intense than any before, my body convulsing with each wave of pleasure.

"Damn, damn, damn," he grumbles, forcefully moving his hips upward, pulling my hips down to match his intense thrusts. With each deep thrust, he hits the end, forcefully penetrating me. Sensing him getting even harder and thicker, I observe him eagerly, wanting to witness his climax. His eyes reflect a wild desire, losing focus as he struggles to maintain control, his beautiful face marked by the relentless pursuit of climax.

"Raya!" He comes with an animalistic release, a snarling ecstasy that captivates me with its intensity. Trembling, he succumbs to the orgasm, his features briefly softening with an unexpected vulnerability.

Holding his face, I gently press my lips against his, offering comfort as the forceful bursts of his gasping breaths touch my cheeks.

"Raya." He envelops me in his arms, embracing me tightly and burying his damp face into the curve of my neck.

Chapter 8

I understand the depth of his emotions. Exposed. Vulnerable.

We linger in that embrace for an extended moment, supporting each other and processing the lingering tremors. He tilts his head and gently kisses me, his tongue's movements in my mouth easing my frayed emotions.

"Amazing," I exhale, affected. His mouth twitches. "Indeed."

I grin, sensing a dazed and euphoric state. Theodore sweeps the damp tendrils of hair off my temples, his fingertips moving almost reverently across my face. The intensity of his gaze makes my chest ache. He appears shocked and...appreciative, his eyes conveying warmth and tenderness. "I don't want to ruin this moment."

Since I sense a 'but' lingering in the air, I ask. "But...?"

"But I can't blow off this meeting. I have a ton of work to do."

"Oh." The moment shatters effectively.

I lift gently off him, biting my lip as he slips wetly out of me. The friction is enough to make me desire more; he's still hard.

"Damn it," he grumbles. "I want to retake you."

He catches me before I slip away, extracting a handkerchief from somewhere and tenderly running it between my legs. It's a profoundly intimate gesture akin to the sex we've just shared.

Once I've dried off, I take a seat on the bed next to him, observing Theodore in silence as he deals with the used condom. He expertly wraps it in a disposable nylon before discreetly disposing of it in a cleverly hidden trash can. After fixing his appearance, he heads into the bathroom for a quick refresh.

After he leaves, I take a shower and wear the oversized shirt and pants he left for me. They're way too big, showing how much bigger he is than me. Breakfast is quiet in Theodore's empty house. The day is long, and since I don't have a job, I walk around the big rooms without purpose.

Maybe it's high time I checked out the place without hating it like I did before.

First, I check out the living room with its fancy furniture and expensive decorations. The sunlight comes through the black velvet drapes, making the pristine Art on the walls look even better. I move to the kitchen, which is super clean and shiny with its steel, modern appliances. The emptiness of the kitchen makes me feel even more alone.

I keep walking and find a cozy library with old books and comfy chairs. There's a grand piano in the corner, waiting for someone to play it. The air smells like old paper, and I remember my strange childhood obsession with old books.

Finally, I find myself standing outside Theodore's study. I feel unsure about invading that personal space but curious, so I go inside. The room is elegant, indicating how organized Theodore is. I look at the shelves with lots of lovely books.

Then, the fact that he'd hidden some papers from me when I came in there the previous day strikes me. The weird feeling from yesterday comes back, making me want to look more. I search through drawers and find a folder with papers about buying companies.

My heart pauses when I see one that's marked 'Kings,' and I grab the document, feeling unsure of what's to come.

ELEVEN.

Theodore.

Sitting through these meetings is a particular brand of torture.

My chest aches each time I see my phone, and I'm overcome with the will to text Raya. I exerted all my self-control to navigate the day without reaching for the phone. I had even sought the help of Fareeda, my assistant, instructing her to physically intervene if it seemed like I might give in to the temptation.

After lengthy discussions with The Lime House and several other places, we managed to strike a deal to collaborate with King's, thanks to William's connections. Although we reached an agreement that works for both sides, I remain cautious. They have a history of questionable actions, and I wouldn't be surprised if they attempt to change certain things when the contracts are finalized.

Till then, I'll keep an eye on them, and then I break the news to Raya

Chapter 8

when everything is done. I wonder what her reaction will be. She'll be overjoyed, but to what extent?

The thought of doing something this special for her brings a wide grin that lasts for the entire day to my face.

When I'm finally free of all the business talk, all I want is to see Raya. To feel her. I quickly make my way back to my car before anyone stops me. As I slip in and start the engine, my phone buzzes with an incoming call from Vicky. I sigh, wondering what she wants from me.

"Hey, Vicky," I answer, trying to keep my tone neutral but planning on ways to keep the conversation brief. The more I talk to her, the longer it takes for me to see Raya.

"Seriously, Theo? Getting back with Raya?" Vicky's voice booms through the phone, and I have to take it away from my ear for a while. I roll my eyes, knowing Eric must've spilled the beans to her.

"Yeah, what's it to you?"

"Seriously, Theo! Remember how that snake broke your heart last time?!" Vicky lectures.

I shrug, not wanting to consider her words. "Water under the bridge. I don't care anymore."

Vicky wasn't convinced. "Are you sure? Eric told me you were just starting to move on."

I hesitate, contemplating her words. Am I making the right choice? After a brief pause, I reply, "Yeah, I'm sure."

Vicky sighs on the other end. "Well, it's your life. Just be cautious, okay?"

That's surprising. Vicky doesn't want to rip my skin off for getting back together with Raya?

"Sure, Vicky," I say dismissively, eager to end the conversation.

After I end the call, I lean back in my seat and sigh. Why did Vicky have to call now and plant a reminder of the past in my head? Now, I feel like I must purge myself of the stain before I go back home to her. I dial Eric. "Meet me at Rover's," I say and hang up without waiting for a response.

With not much else happening, I decided to hit up Eric, and we drove our asses to the cozy Irish pub off Sixth. The place is a bit cramped, but luckily, we snag two empty spots at the bar.

"I'll go for whiskey on the rocks," Eric tells the bartender. "What about you?"

"Not really in the mood for a drink," I reply, fully aware that Eric won't let that slide.

He straightens up, locking eyes with me. "You don't want a drink?" Giving me a quick once-over, he grows serious. "Dude, are you unwell? Like, do you have some sort of disease? A terminal illness?"

"No." I roll my eyes. "I just don't want one, okay?" Checking my watch once more, I count down the minutes.

"Something is going on. Throughout my lifetime of knowing you, not once have you ever shaken your head to a drink. What's up? Is something going on that I don't know about?"

"No. I'm just not in the mood to drink. Will you please let this one slide?"

"Can't." Eric shakes his head, lips tightly pressed together. "Sorry, but —" He pauses, and his eyes suddenly sparkle. Oh, man. Sometimes, I genuinely dislike how incredibly perceptive this guy is. It didn't take him up to a minute to figure me out. "You've got feelings for Raya Kings, don't you?"

Seriously, nothing escapes this guy's notice.

I won't even bother denying it. Instead, I lean against the bar, clasping my hands together. "Yeah, I am."

"And she's one of the good ones, right?"

"Considering she once broke up with me because of my lifestyle, yeah."

"Wow," Eric exclaims in amazement. "I can't believe you found a girl who can rein you in."

"She's not reining me in," I reply, growing weary of this discussion. "I'm just aiming to make a difference, you know? Putting in effort."

"You do fine as you are, but you're mellowing and dialing it down." He

Chapter 8

raises his glass to me. "Good for you. I'm happy to see you're not living the live-fast-and-die-hard life. I'd prefer to have my cousin around for a while before he kicks the bucket."

"If I haven't kicked the bucket yet, I doubt I ever will."

Smirking, Eric agrees. "It's eerie how accurate that is, but for real, you're in love with her?"

"Yeah."

"For real?" The amusement in Eric's tone fades as he questions, "When did this happen?"

"That's the crazy part." I laugh. "I have no idea."

"What brought it on?"

I adjust on my bar stool, feeling a strain in my knees from the awkward angle.

"I honestly don't know, dude." I rub my jaw. "I couldn't shake her from my thoughts. I tried, believe me, but each effort only intensified my desire for her. Even though it's scary, and I've never been through this, I knew there was no way I could walk away. There's something about her that I can't quite figure out, making me incredibly desperate whenever she's near."

A knowing grin appears on his face. "You're done for."

"I am. I truly, deeply love her." I exhale deeply. "Damn, listen to a dickhead like me being all sappy in love."

"Just the mention of love makes me want to puke." He takes a swig of his drink and then places it on the bar.

"What's going on with us? First Vicky, now you. What happened to being the hot, single billionaire cousins for life?"

"Aren't you with that Ciara girl?"

"Nah." He dismisses it with a wave. "She was just a good time; nothing serious there."

"Still holding out for whom you say we shouldn't talk about?" I wink at him, and he groans in frustration.

"When I say we shouldn't talk about her, I mean, as a whole, don't even bring up that fact that I don't want us to talk about her. Damn it, man."

"You're so touchy." I poke his shoulder. "Relax."

"When did this turn into my problem? We were discussing your love life and the fact that you're deeply in love with a woman who once broke your heart. Besides, you did intend to assist her company, double her connection to the place, and then betray her by taking it from her. How do you plan to handle that?"

"I've decided to let that go." I shrug as my phone vibrates. "There are plenty of other companies to purchase."

I expected a part of me to feel bad about finally coming to terms with that, but I'm disappointed. I feel okay—superb, in fact—about letting Kings go. There's no way in the world I'll ever forgive myself if I hurt Raya. But we'll see. I pull out my phone and see that it's a text from Raya. "Looks like I have to go." I pat Eric on the back. "I'll see you later."

"Wait, you're just going to leave me here?"

"Um, yeah?"

I pat Eric's shoulder lightly and stride out of the place. The man must be cursing me under his breath, but I'm too excited to care. Raya wants me to come home. She says she needs to talk to me. Maybe it's finally time for us to talk about all of this. She'd admit her undying affection for me, and I'd do the same and relieve her of the nanny duties. Finally, we'd make mind-blowing love and cement our bond. However, these plans won't exactly make any sense without flowers involved, so I make a quick stop at a nearby flower shop.

I scan the colorful array of blooms, searching for the right bouquet. Roses, they say, convey emotions like nothing else. I hesitate for a moment, then reach for a bunch of red roses, their vibrant petals standing out against the sea of flowers. Clutching the bouquet, I can't shake the knot of anxiety in my chest.

As I walk back to the car, the roses in hand, I quickly rehearse some lines I got off the internet. And thanks to my photographic memory, I'm already reciting the entire paragraph when I'm only halfway home.

Chapter 8

Arriving home, I hold the roses tightly, hoping they will serve as a peace offering. Opening the door, I expect a usual welcome, maybe a smile or a warm hug. Instead, I am met with Raya's furious gaze.

She is standing in the living room, her eyes ablaze with an anger that hits me like a punch to the gut. The rose suddenly grows thorns that prickle me even though they're securely wrapped in a shiny red gift nylon.

"What's the matter, Raya?" I venture, my voice carrying a note of confusion. "I got you these roses. Thought it would be a nice gesture."

Her scowl deepens as she swiftly spins on her heels and storms inside. I follow her, an uneasy feeling growing with each step. The atmosphere is charged with so much tension, and I don't know why.

Raya enters my study and returns with an overfamiliar file, one that holds the truth I had hoped to keep hidden a little longer. She flings it at me with a force that catches me off guard. I barely manage to dodge the file, and the roses in my hand end up slightly crumpled.

"Whoa, what's going on?" I exclaim, still holding the roses, which are now less of a gesture and more of a wilted apology.

"You know exactly what's going on," Raya retorts, her voice thick with anger. "You've been playing games with me, Theo."

The realization hits me like a tidal wave. She thinks I'm still going through with it. She points at the file on the floor, her eyes demanding an explanation.

"This! My company. The one I've put my heart and soul into. You were going to take it away from me, and you never bothered to tell me," she accuses. "Have you just been playing me?"

I've never seen Raya burn with so much rage before. It scares me so bad that I drop the roses and close the distance between us.

"Look, Raya, I promise it's not what you think."

But she isn't ready to listen. The half-truth she has discovered has blindsided her, and the roses that I thought would bring solace feel feeble in the face of her justified anger.

"Don't even try to explain. You've been hiding this, playing with my feelings, and now you think a bouquet of roses will fix everything?" Her words cut through me, and I struggled to find the proper response.

"Raya, please, let me explain. It's not as bad as you think," I plead.

But Raya, fueled by betrayal and hurt, storms out of the study and ignores all of my attempts to call her back. She enters her room, throws the closet door open, and starts to throw her things in a bag.

For the first time, I feel fear. It's in its raw form, tearing into my heart ravenously.

"Raya, what are you doing?"

"What does it look like I'm doing?" She fires back as she continues to throw random things in the bag.

"I wasn't going through with it! Please let me explain."

"Explain? I trusted you, Theo. I believed in us. But you've been keeping this from me. Is it some sort of sick payback plan you had in your head? What, just when I start to be happy, you'll take it away from me? How could you?"

Desperation takes over. "I care about you! It's not just about the company. There's more to it."

She scoffs, a bitter laugh escaping her. "Save your explanations. I believed in you, and you stabbed me in the back. That's all."

I reach out to touch her arm gently, hoping for a connection amid the chaos, but she recoils, eyes ablaze with fury. "Don't touch me. I can't believe I trusted you. Packs of roses or not, I'm done, Theo. I won't stay where I'm not wanted. I can't trust you anymore," she declares, slinging her bag over her shoulder. "And don't you dare come after me."

With that, she storms out of the place, leaving me standing there stunned. I'm afraid I've just lost the only woman in the whole world who's ever meant anything to me, and as she walks out of my house—and possibly my life forever—I can do nothing to bring her back.

TWELVE

Raya.

"Goooood morn—holy Mary, mother of God," Kaylee exclaims when I look up at her. "Ummm," she leans toward me and whispers as she quickly

Chapter 8

glances around the coffee house—"do you realize you literally look like death right now?"

"Is that so?" I reply with sarcasm, placing my coffee cup on the table as Kaylee joins me, holding her to-go cup. "I was under the impression I resembled a poised debutante when I left the house this morning."

Kaylee shakes her head. "Take another look in the mirror, Raya. I adore you, but you appear like a Barbie doll that's been through a rough night being dragged all over the train tracks."

"You're very kind."

"I apologize, but when have I ever been honest with you?"

"I understand, but you could at least finish saying good morning before poking fun at me."

"I'm sorry," she says sincerely. "I was caught off guard. I'm going to guess it has something to do with the same reason you had me pick you up from his place, and you slammed my door in my face once we got to your place?"

"About that ..." I start to say, remorseful. I may look like shit right now, but I feel like it more.

This morning, it took three shots and four swishes of mouthwash to prepare for the day. Now, with sunglasses covering my eyes and a thick scruff concealing my bruised jaw, I sit in the back, holding a cup of coffee. Leaning into the booth, I close my eyes, hoping the pounding headache attacking my skull eases so I can make it through this meeting without tossing my cookies.

For the first time in my life, I drank until I blacked out. Last night, I came across the notepad in which I wrote my New Year's resolutions. We're still in the early months of the year, and everything I listed out seems like an exaggerated joke, especially the last item.

1. Experience life to the fullest.
2. Sample all the iconic foods in New York City.
3. Hit up a nightclub for a night out.
4. Lose myself in Central Park for a day.
5. Fall in love.

Yes, that last one brought tears to my eyes.

I can mark it done. I fell in love, and I fell hard. If only that love had been mutual. When I wrote that resolution, I envisioned finding someone eager to spend a lifetime together. I never foresaw ending up with a shattered heart courtesy of a man with soulful eyes that penetrate the soul.

Now, I'm stuck with swollen eyes, a sore throat, and a massive hangover that has me dragging even worse than before.

"Look, Kaylee. I'm so sorry for the way I acted. Thanks for picking me up that night. I couldn't have handled driving then."

"Of course, Raya. I'm here for you." Kaylee reaches out and takes my hand in hers, her eyes softening. "You looked really upset. It tore at my heart, but I didn't want to push you off the edge. Do you want to talk about it now?"

I sigh, my free hand's fingers nervously tapping on my lap. Then I nod as Kaylee moves away but leaves her hand resting on mine, offering her reassurance without trying to overwhelm me—a top woman, for real. "I don't even know where to start. It's just all so complicated."

"Well, start wherever you feel comfortable. I'm here to listen."

"I moved out of Theo's place. I saw these documents in his study, and now I'm a mess. I don't know what to do."

"Maybe it would help to talk it out. What happened?"

I gaze out the window, my voice shaky. "He was planning to take the company from me after we get it back on its feet. I confronted him, but he claimed it was never his plan. But, Kaylee ...," My voice breaks. "The papers were right there with me. I touched them. How could I take his words over what I could see?"

Kaylee, ever the supportive friend, listens intently. "My goodness, that's a lot to take in. If you physically saw those papers, it's understandable that you'd question his intentions. But have you considered having a direct conversation with Theo about this? Maybe there's more to the story that you're not aware of."

I let out a heavy sigh. "I don't know. Right now, I'm just ... I'm caught

Chapter 8

up in this whirlwind of emotions. I'm angry, hurt, and confused all at once. I can't trust my judgment when it comes to him."

"Trust is a tricky thing," Kaylee replies, her voice gentle. "But you've got to communicate if you want any clarity. Maybe he has a valid explanation, or perhaps there's been a misunderstanding. Keeping it bottled up won't do you any good."

"I don't even know if I can bring myself to talk to him."

Kaylee reaches again. This time, her hand offers a comforting touch on my shoulder. "Girl, you're strong, and you've faced challenges before. If you decide to confront him, take it at your own pace. But closure can be healing, even if it's painful at first," She says. "And if you need someone to talk to or if you want me to be there when you confront him, just say the word. I'm here for you, no matter what."

I sip my coffee quietly, feeling Kaylee's eyes pressing into me.

"Spill," I tell her, and she doesn't hesitate.

"Well, I was just thinking ... maybe giving Theo a chance to explain himself could be a good idea. Hear him out."

"I don't think I can. It's not that simple. I just know I'll go running back into his hands once the first word is out of his mouth. Every time I'm around him, I feel this pull, this unexplainable force that draws me to him. It's like I'm falling hopelessly in love with him again, and it terrifies me."

"Love can be scary, but it can also be beautiful. Maybe there's a reason you feel drawn to him. Have you considered giving it another try?"

I shake my head, my eyes clouded with uncertainty. "I left to protect myself. Getting back with him would be like walking into a disaster. I can't risk it."

"Raya, people can change. Maybe Theo has changed, too. You won't know unless you listen to what he has to say."

"I've heard it all before," I say, rolling my eyes. "Promises, apologies, declarations of love. But what happens when the dust settles? We end up back where we started."

"It's true that actions speak louder than words. Maybe he's learned from the past. You deserve happiness, and if there's a chance for that with Theo, it might be worth considering."

"I can't. I've worked so hard to rebuild my life after everything fell apart. Going back to him feels like unraveling all that progress."

"You have to do what's right for you, girl. If going back to him doesn't feel right, then trust your instincts."

"I am. Leaving is the right thing to do. I need to focus on myself and my future, not get tangled up in the mess of our past."

Kaylee reaches over to give my hand a reassuring squeeze. "Whatever you decide, I'm here for you. Just remember, you deserve to be happy, no matter what that looks like," she tells me. "And, I understand this might not be what you want to hear, but love has its unpredictable ways. It can whisk you away, creating beautiful moments that feel like a sunset. Yet, there are times when love serves as a lesson, a brief chapter in the grand story of your life. Take your time, absorb the lessons from the love you shared, and eventually, the ache in your chest will soften, and the world around you will regain its vibrant colors."

Even as I acknowledge the truth in her words and recognize that time may heal, there's a profound realization within me that I won't easily let go of this love. This was the first instance where someone became intertwined with the very essence of my being. A part of my existence will forever bear the imprint of Theodore Caddel, and it's a reality I'll carry with me for the entirety of my life.

THIRTEEN.

Theo

"What are you wearing?" Eric questions, eyeing my clothes as I take a seat at the table. "And why the sudden departure from the couch? Have you finally grown tired of sulking around?"

I undo the buttons on my suit coat and reach for the cufflinks laid out on the table before me. "It's a suit, and just be quiet, okay?"

"Sure, it's obviously a suit, but you've got a tie on. You never wear ties. You usually leave the top buttons undone to flaunt your broad chest, or whatever it is that gets your women on their knees," he points at my neatly

Chapter 8

knotted tie. "And you're in grey, whereas it's always black on you. Why are you in grey?" He leans back in his chair and gives me a thorough once-over. "Your beard is strangely trimmed. It started to grow since you wouldn't shave. And now, your eyes aren't bloodshot."

He takes in the changes, and I give him the time to do so.

"You don't have the scent of alcohol on you," he remarks, still processing.

"You've had a haircut. You appear refreshed."

And once again...

"Holy Shit."

Yeah, there it is. His eyes bulge out of his sockets. "Are you planning to win her back?"

"I believe so."

"You think so?" Eric abandons his chair and positions himself directly in front of me.

"What are your plans? What prompted this change of heart? I thought you'd thrown in the towel and consigned yourself to misery. Are you considering proposing?"

"Easy there." I meet his gaze. "I'm nowhere near proposing. I need to ensure she's open to ... you know, dating me after I acted like a total dick to her."

"Just give her your charming smile, throw in a 'baby girl' with a heavy accent, and then go in for a passionate kiss. Easy."

"Not even you would follow that advice," I reply without emotion.

He grins. "Yeah, that's terrible advice. But seriously, what happened? What made you reconsider? Last I checked, you were practically dying on that couch for a week."

Eric is correct, but I'm not about to let him rain on my parade. After Raya left, my world crumbled. Nights turned into a blurry haze of alcohol, and the echo of her laughter haunts my every thought. I crashed at Eric's place because I saw Raya's face and smelled her in every room in my house.

I spent days on the couch, drowning my sorrows in whiskey, hoping the burn of alcohol would replace the ache in my chest. I avoided mirrors, unable to face the reflection that mocked the man who let the love of his life slip away.

I refused to eat, and sleep eluded me as if mocking my inability to escape the torment, even in dreams. In the silence of the night, I'd hear her voice, see her face, and feel the void she had left behind.

And for the first time, I cried.

I cried for the loss, for the mistakes that pushed her away, and for the unbearable emptiness that engulfed me. The weight of my actions pressed down on me like a heavy burden, and I felt the crushing reality of what I had done.

I avoided everyone, locking myself in a self-imposed exile. Colleagues called, and work piled up, but I couldn't find the strength to respond. The world outside seemed distant like I no longer belonged there.

Eric watched my descent into despair. He tried to pull me back, offering comfort and advice, but my heart remained trapped in the ruins of what it once was.

But just last night, I saw a glimmer of clarity through the haze of my grief. It wasn't a sudden revelation but a gradual realization that I couldn't continue like this. Raya's absence was a void, but my self-destruction wouldn't bring her back.

As I stood in Eric's living room and got ready to win Raya back, I acknowledged the pain but also the resilience that brought me back from the brink.

Life without Raya was a challenge, and now, my determination to mend what I'd broken is driving me to her place, taking me up to her front door, and having me knock on the door without losing my courage.

Raya answers on the third knock.

"Theo?" Raya calls, disbelief evident in her voice, her words catching in her throat.

"R–Raya. You're home."

"Yeah," she replies awkwardly, my nerves churning in my stomach. "Did you, um, need something?"

Chapter 8

Taking a step forward, my hand tightens at the back of my neck. "I was hoping we could talk."

"Sure," she says, moving aside and allowing me into her apartment.

Don't set yourself up for disappointment, Theo. It might mean nothing.

Walking past her, my eyes briefly catch the yellow plaid shorts and matching top she's wearing. How she manages to look adorable in those is beyond me.

After closing the door, I turn around and finally get a good look at her face. Her cheeks are tinged with pink, and her eyes are red and swollen. The realization hits me hard – I've deeply wounded her. I am the cause of her tears. Damn, I feel like dog food material right now.

Raya catches my gaze as I observe her, and she quickly explains, saying, "I, um... had something in my eye."

"Seems like it." Leaning against the door, I nervously rub my hands against my clothes, uncertain about the next move. My initial instinct urges me to embrace her and kiss away the distress on her face. The second instinct is trying to push me to kneel and apologize sincerely for causing her pain.

"Shall we sit down?"

"I prefer standing, but if you want to sit, go ahead," she replies.

Sitting is the last thing on my mind, especially when my heart seems to be pounding in my throat. Scanning the room, I notice a notepad on her nightstand. It appears she has a list, specifically a New Year's resolution. My stomach sinks as I read her final resolution, which states, 'Fall in love,' and it's marked as complete.

Pointing at the notebook involuntarily, I ask, "What's that?"

In a few swift steps, Raya reaches for the notebook, closes it, and tosses it onto the floor. "Nothing. It's nothing at all."

Pressing further, I ask, "Raya, what was that?"

"Nothing that concerns you."

"Don't lie to me."

"Lie to you?" Her voice rises in volume. "Like you have room to talk. If you want to talk about the truth, why don't you start?"

Ouch.

"Alright," I declare with certainty in my voice as I narrow the distance between us. "I apologize for causing you pain. I feel remorse for not being the man you needed when you needed a shoulder to cry on. I am sorry for sowing doubt about the importance of our relationship." I gently press her against the door. "And I regret that it took me this long to realize that, despite my errors, you're the one meant for me." I cradle her cheek as tears flow down, tears of genuine joy. "I love you, Raya, and I want you not to doubt that moving forward."

I hadn't realized the immense need to express those words until I finally did. My love for Raya is profound, and the desire for her is so intense it's almost painful.

Raya buries her face in her hand, closing her eyes, savoring the sensation of my presence, relishing the contact.

When she opens her eyes, she declares, "You fucker, why did it take you so long? I love you too, Theodore."

These words are the most exquisite in the world. I've yearned to hear them, and it feels like a burden has been lifted from my chest. Now, I'm at ease enough for a smirk to grace my face. "So, that fallen-in-love box you ticked on your list, was that about me?"

She affirms, "It was, but when I marked that checkbox, I never anticipated nursing a broken heart simultaneously."

"I'm sorry, baby girl," I murmur, drawing her into my chest and enveloping her in my arms. One of my hands supports the back of her head as I press my lips against her hair. "I'm so sincerely sorry. I wasn't in a good place. I've only recently pulled myself from the self-inflicted state of self-loathing I subjected myself to. I intended to wait until I felt complete enough for you, but then I realized I wouldn't truly be whole until I had you back in my life again."

"You don't need to strive for perfection, Theodore." She raises her head, locking eyes with me.

Chapter 8

"I love you because you're imperfect because you have rough edges. I love you because you're the one who makes me feel at home. When I'm in your arms, surrounded by your warmth, everything feels right, and I never want to live without that."

"Hmm, fair."

"Or ... "Raya says, pulling back. There's a glint in her eye. "Maybe I should just do this instead."

"You won't." I press another kiss to her head, enveloping her in another embrace. "I refuse to let you slip away again, Raya Kings."

A smile plays on her lips. "Is that a promise?"

"Should I shout in capitals to make it clearer?"

"I suppose so." Raya laughs, tracing her hand up my chest to the buttons of my shirt. "I guess that means you'll have to yell it."

"Or ..." Raya pulls away, her eyes twinkling. "Maybe I should just do this instead."

My gaze narrows, and in an instant, her lips are on my neck, and her hands roam across my body, undressing me completely.

As Raya plants tender kisses along my neck, I appreciate that love, even in difficult moments, possesses the power to mend profound wounds. Without it, I wouldn't comprehend the essence of true love—the beautiful and the ugly.

THE END

Epilogue

Thank you for reading **Nanny for My Billionaire Ex**.

If you liked this book, you'll love **Billionaire's Fake Engagement**.

It's a steamy story about finding the man of your dreams for the second time around; this time, he comes with baggage ... The happy ending will leave you satisfied but ready for more...

Click here to get Billionaire's Fake Engagement!

Here's a sneak peek...
In the heart of my new town, I find myself drawn to a familiar face—my billionaire ex from college.

Epilogue

It seems fate has a twisted sense of humor; he's now my next-door neighbor.

Our history is stormy, but now, I see a different side to him—a devoted father with a charming demeanor.

He is still the most charming man I have ever met.

One innocent coffee date leads to an electric, satisfying night.

Before I know it, I'm captivated for a second time.

But a part of me wonders, is this real, or am I just falling for the same old charm?

And as we spend more time together, I yearn for a family with him and his adorable son Jacob.

But there's a catch—Jacob's future hangs in the balance.

Luke asks me to be his fake fiance to secure Jacob's place in the best preschool.

With so much at stake this time, I hope I don't regret giving my college ex a second chance.

This forced proximity, second-chance romance is a heartwarming tale sprinkled with humor, passion, and a dash of Daddy duty. Get ready to swoon, laugh, and fall head over heels in this sizzling enemies-to-lovers romance filled with witty banter, steamy tension, and surprises!

Click here to get Billionaire's Fake Engagement!

Billionaire's Fake Engagement

I*n the heart of my new town, I find myself drawn to a familiar face—my billionaire ex from college.*

It seems fate has a twisted sense of humor; he's now my next-door neighbor.

Our history is stormy, but now, I see a different side to him—a devoted father with a charming demeanor.

He is still the most charming man I have ever met.

One innocent coffee date leads to an electric, satisfying night.

Before I know it, I'm captivated for a second time.

But a part of me wonders, is this real, or am I just falling for the same old charm?

As we spend more time together, I yearn for a family with him and his adorable son Jacob.

But there's a catch—Jacob's future hangs in the balance.

Luke asks me to be his fake fiance to secure Jacob's place in the best preschool.

I accept, but with so much at stake this time, I hope I don't regret giving my college ex a second chance.

. . .

Chapter 1
ONE:
Theodore

The sound of the door opening distracts me for a moment.

The intruder pokes a head in first.

I lift a hand to stop Miss Jones from saying anything further.

Schooling my face from expressing surprise at the first sight of her after so many years, I lean back on my chair.

"Miss Jones, leave us."

Miss Jones nods, grabs a couple of files, and hurries away.

I note the surprise in her eyes with amusement. Surely, she can't be surprised to see me here. Nervous maybe.

"Ray," I comment, the name feeling strange in my mouth.

How long has it been? Ten years?

My eyes roam over her. Dressed in an impeccable scoop-neck knee-length green dress, she looks prim and proper, unlike the carefree and jovial girl in college.

"It's Raya, Mr. Caddel."

I smirk at her attempt at forced formality.

I stretch forth a hand. "Please, have a seat."

Leaning forward, I rest my elbows on the desk. I study Raya's profile, noting with pride how age has done little to nothing to her appearance. She's still as gorgeous as ever, and of course, ever the smart mouth.

"What brings you here?"

Did she get wind of my plans?

Click here to get Billionare's Fake Engagement now!